surrender to you

NEW YORK TIMES BESTSELLING AUTHOR

SHAWNTELLE MADISON

Copyright © 2016 by Shawntelle Madison

Second Electronic Printing: Copyright © 2018 Shawntelle Madison

Print Edition: Copyright © 2018 Shawntelle Madison

First Printing: July 2018

ISBN-13: 978-0-9966701-6-6

eISBN-13: 978-0-9966701-7-3

Cover design: The Killion Group, Inc.

Chapter One

_____

Carlie

L ess than six hours after arriving in Boston from London, and I couldn't keep still: tonight I had penciled in plans for a party in Booty Call Land. For the fourth time, I switched from leaning on one leg to the other. A light tickle along my inner thighs from the ribbons on my garters made me ache further. I didn't have much longer until cocktail hour at the Subarctic Club.

First things first though, before I could get a drink and be rid of this pent-up sexual tension, I had to make some arrangements.

"How do you plan to pay for the room, Miss Jason?" the front desk clerk at the Bellevue Hotel asked. My cell-phone sang the chorus from M.I.A's "_Bad Girls_," but I ignored it.

"American Express, please." Before I'd walked into the opulent lobby with its marble floors and red carpets, I'd considered the answer to this question. My American Express black card had enough credit for a month's stay, as long as that stay didn't include room service, overseas calls, or extravagant perks like raiding the minibar for Milky Ways.

As he completed my registration, the front desk clerk was all smiles. More than five years ago, I'd started out as a hotel concierge. Back then, the eagerness to please oozed out of my pores. Every happy customer meant a positive review or a possible promotion. Working at a five-star hotel in NYC was like that. Maybe that was the reason why I ended up opening my own personal concierge business.

The clerk finished my transaction, handed me a keycard, and gave me the standard spiel. "Is there anything else I can help you with?" he added.

"Thanks, Frank, you've been more than helpful." Working the front desk was a thankless job. Everyone came to you with their problems—plugged up toilets, complaints about the couple next door screaming out expletives during sex—but you always had to appear calm and polite. Even if you weren't feeling it.

After I settled into my room, I finally returned the call from earlier. This particular person wouldn't be satisfied with a text message.

"What's wrong now, *Penny*?" I asked with a sigh.

"What's wrong is you got back from the UK, stopped at my place, hung out with Sophie, and then didn't wait for me to come home."

I rolled my eyes. At least she wasn't in front of me right now. There would be over-the-top hand gestures involved and head rolling. As one of my best friends since our days in the foster care system, I loved Penny dearly, but once you ticked her off, you heard about it for weeks. At least, Sophie was far more levelheaded.

Relaxing was out of the question, so I decided to chat with Penny on the way to a coffee shop across the street from the hotel. Downtown Boston buzzed around me, making it hard to hear our conversation.

Even this early in the afternoon, Penny continued to berate me with that saccharine voice of hers. "If you weren't staying in town for a while, I would've snatched your fake-blonde ass off the street and beat you down for ignoring one of your besties."

Umm, thank you? "Oh, don't be mad you can't pull off blonde."

"I know you're joking, but have you ever seen a blonde Indian chick? The men come running, sweetie. So where are you going and when are we hanging out?"

"We can have breakfast tomorrow, if you want." Yep, I dodged her question.

"When have you ever seen me up early enough for breakfast?"

Never, which was why I suggested it. "Look, I'm borderline jet-lagged, so by tomorrow morning I can tell you *whatever* you want."

"Why tomorrow morning? Why can't you stay here with Sophie and me?"

"And sleep on your couch for a week?" I chuckled. "No thanks." I had a whirlpool bathtub, and I planned to make good use of it.

"I have a queen-sized bed——" she began.

"I'm good, girl." *Not happening.* Doing the roommate thing with her for over ten years as a kid was enough.

"So where are you going?" Penny was a pro at poking in my business.

"To get some coffee so I can wake up."

She took a deep breath. "You're not seeing *him*, are you?"

Now that made me stop in the middle of the crosswalk.

A car honked at me, forcing me to keep going. She knew me all too well.

"You are a little freak of the week," Penny chirped.

"Oh, *stop* it."

"My thoughts exactly. Does Sophie know you're about to hook up with Tomas again?"

Of course, Sophie didn't know. If Penny hadn't pried, I'd be able to shove whatever happened tonight into a pretty little box I could hide under my bed.

She kept going. "You two need to stop doing this. I'm all for casual sex every now and then, but hooking up with the same person every couple of years is saying something."

"Maybe it means we like to *fuck* each other?" An approaching lady, who appeared to be around my age, flashed me a dirty look for cursing. I didn't see any sensitive young ears skittering about.

Penny laughed into the phone. "No, it means you two can't commit, and you care about each other."

This little speech wasn't new. Sophie and Penny lectured me every chance they could get.

"You two keep running away from each other, only to end up back together," Penny said. "Maybe he's waiting for you to stop running?"

I held back a snort. "Tomas isn't *waiting* for anyone. Nor has he ever waited for me after we had sex. We both get what we want and we move on. Like we should do with this conversation."

"Fine, but I'm calling you extra *early* tomorrow morning just because I can."

"Bring it, babe." Penny slept like the dead. She wasn't calling anybody...

∾

TWO HOURS LATER, after somehow getting off the phone with Penny, the sun had set, and now I weaved through the crowded floor at the Subarctic Club in downtown Boston. The heavy bass to the pop music thrummed through my bones. Just another night of partying for the young and elite. Out of all the places I could've selected, I considered this neutral ground. Tomas wasn't the kind of guy to seek out the flashing lights or the bubble-gum, sunshine electronic music blasting through the speakers. He was more of a jazz or big-band club kind of guy. Give him smooth music and I'd be the one playing into his hands.

But not tonight.

I made my way to the bar on the other side of the huge rectangular room. Shelves with beautiful sparkling liquor bottles and dark blue lights extended from the bar below to the ceiling above. This was my first time visiting the place, but I liked the overall nautical vibe.

With so many people here, it was hard to avoid prying eyes. Whether the dancer was a man or a woman, their first glance was what usually enchanted me. A beautiful half-Asian, half-black girl danced suggestively with a group of friends. She looked at me over her shoulder and her face blossomed into a smile. As pretty as she was though, tonight wasn't about playing, but finding a place to wait for Tomas. Just the thought of seeing him made my stomach quiver.

I moved faster. Anticipation snaked up my back. I scanned the bar to find a place to slide in. The club was pretty packed, so I had to walk a bit. One man smiled my way and gestured for me to take his place so he could stand behind me.

No thanks. I shook my head. Repaying the favor wasn't happening. I kept going until I spotted a man leaving the bar holding a few shots. He hurried back to his table of friends, and I took his place.

Once I slid onto the warmed leather seat, I sighed. There wasn't a place like this in London. I only had to close my eyes to hear the sounds of the Northeast. In just this one club, I could hear accents that only existed in the US. Technically, I was more of New York City girl, but I could learn to love Boston based on what I'd seen so far.

The bartender approached me. "What are you having tonight?"

I hesitated at my choice, but gave in. No more vodka for me. Back in London I learned I had Celiac disease. "Two shots of tequila and coke, please. No ice."

"Coming right up."

Time passed, but not much. Maybe it seemed as if I sat there for a long time, but I hadn't. The moment the seat next to mine opened up, Tomas Goodfellow slid in beside me. My breath caught in my chest and a hum settled in the back of my throat. As much as I wanted to focus on the bartender, who flipped shot glasses and placed them in a perfect row for his cheering customers, my body always reacted the moment I saw Tomas.

Not a single person close to us suspected they drank next to one of the richest hoteliers in the world. He was just Tomas to me.

I sucked in a deep breath. Memories of his strong citrus scent with a hint of spice flared in my mind. I could pick out the individual flavors: ginger, bergamot, cardamom, along with a hint of grapefruit and lavender. Damn, he always smelled good enough to eat.

Just one peek wouldn't hurt.

Eyes forward, Carlie. Of course, I failed miserably and looked at him briefly. My eyes drank him in from the curve of his strong jawline to his dark brown eyes. *And his lips.*

Tomas had the kind of lips that were meant to be sampled. They were sensuously shaped, practically mocking me while I stared. When I turned my head just right, I could make out the slight upward tilt in his lips.

The bartender asked if he wanted anything.

"Vanilla vodka, please. Two shots," he said.

He ordered our usual.

Somehow, even though we sat next to each other, our bodies didn't touch. The edge of his arm, where firm muscles bulged from underneath his dark gray shirt, was mere inches from mine. An itch formed along that tiny patch of my skin. He radiated warmth and the need to slide into his arms grew overwhelming.

Tomas finished his first shot quickly while I continued to sip mine.

"I've been watching you from across the room," he said to me, a hint of his Portuguese accent touching his words. He had the kind of voice that slid up your inner thighs.

"Are you a stalker or something?" I whispered.

"Would you like for me to be?" His eyebrows lowered, and a dark smirk filled his face.

I smiled as he extended his hand toward me. "I'm Tomas. What's your name?"

"Grace." Choosing my name for the evening was a game we played once in a while. So far I'd only picked virtuous names by alphabet: Amity, Charity, and now Grace.

"Do you come here often?" He gestured for the bartender to bring him another drink.

"Never been."

His arm finally brushed against mine as he leaned closer. "Interesting choice."

He asked me what I was doing in town, and as usual, I kept things vague. I was on a personal trip to find someone important and I needed a drink to settle my nerves. Which was the truth.

"Have you found what you're looking for yet?" he asked me smoothly.

Does he mean my search for my parents or my desire to see him tonight?

Faintly, I felt his fingertips press on the middle of my back. A light caress meant to tease. I needed much more than that tonight.

"Not yet." All this small talk was nice, but my patience was running out.

Down the bar, a group of women were eyeing Tomas. They smiled repeatedly and pointed in his direction. The countdown began until a drink would come his way. He had that effect on other women. Just like he did on me. What made me different though was I told myself I didn't care.

Less than a minute later, a glass of expensive brandy appeared—along with a business card with a phone number. "From the ladies over in the corner," the bartender said, "with their compliments."

"Show-off," I couldn't help but whisper.

"Have you had any drinks bought for you yet?" Tomas replied.

"The night is young. Sooner or later, someone will become brave enough to buy me a drink, but I think we should go somewhere quiet before the cougar club comes prowling your way."

I turned my head toward his, trying to keep myself from falling for him. The intensity of his gaze had a way of making me succumb every time.

"We should." He placed a few bills on the bar to pay for both of our drinks.

Somehow, I added distance between us. For a fleeting

moment, I told myself to walk away. If I were smart, I would've already buried my feelings as deeply as he did.

"Let's go then," I said.

I left first and he trailed behind me. Not once did he touch me. We left the Subarctic Club and made our way to the busy street. A Maserati sedan waited at the curb. Silence settled between us as we slipped inside. This was the game we always played. No polite conversation to ask how the other was doing or even a dinner to set the mood.

All these things were my own fault, though.

I was the one who made Tomas this way.

Chapter Two

Tomas

The moment Carlie's text message flashed on my phone—after four years no less—I didn't hesitate to clear my schedule. Every message she'd sent me over the years had been this simple: *flight to Boston arrives at 11 am. subarctic club at 8 pm.*

Her messages always meant only one thing: *meet and fuck.*

As much as I traveled, I was surprised she knew I was here.

The woman next to me in the car shifted, placing one leg over the other. My gaze drifted up the perfect curve of her calves to the place where her garter ribbons peeked out from under her short, leather skirt. Grace, as she'd called herself this time, watched the brownstone buildings we passed as we drove further into downtown Boston. In the darkness of the Maserati, I could still make out every feature. Even if I closed my eyes, I could clearly recall everything about her. The dimple in her cheek when she truly smiled. The dark shine to her olive-green eyes when she saw something she wanted. But her hair color was all wrong. How she thought blonde hair was better than her natural red, I didn't know, but this was Carlie, after all. She jumped in head-first for everything. On closer inspection, I noticed she was thinner than usual. Had she been working too much?

The makeup she wore covered all the endearing light brown freckles that dotted her face and trailed down her neck and back. Countless times I'd kissed that skin, commanded her with a single glance to fall to her knees so I could twine my hands in her curly, red hair and draw her mouth to my cock. My fingers on my right hand gripped my knee tighter. The need to reach for her grew stronger. Only a few inches separated us, but now wasn't the time to make my move.

Soon enough, my lazy moment taking her in came to an end. We reached the destination Carlie had given the driver: the Fulbright Hotel. I smiled at her choice. She'd picked one of my competitors. The dark interior of the car was suddenly illuminated from all the lights blanketing the entrance.

The bellman opened the door and offered his hand to help her out. Then, it was just me and her walking side by side. Every once in a while, her arm brushed against mine and a sense of déjà vu crept in. We'd walked this path before in another place and another time. The apex of these events was the always same: we ended up in bed.

And yet, standing this close to her left my stomach muscles tense, my breath quickening and my heart racing. We reached the elevator, and the doors opened not long after I pressed the button. Instead of an empty cab, a family of seven took up most of the space. The parents beckoned an older boy and what looked to be his girlfriend, along with three younger kids, to make some room. We shuffled inside and took a spot in the left corner. Ironically, we faced each other, nearly nose to nose, with little room to budge. Her back was to the wall and I practically caged her in.

She was right where I wanted her.

She looked up at me and bit her upper lip. A pout. I glanced downward, watching the way she tilted forward a bit until I could see down the front of her black blouse. *No bra this time.*

This elevator was going too slow.

"*Maman,* when are we going to the aquarium?" the little girl asked the older woman in French.

"Stop asking," the older boy grated. "We just got here."

Carlie glanced at the boy's hand clutching his girlfriend's. A genuine smile touched the corner of her mouth and the dimple she hid most of the time with her impassive expressions appeared. Now that was the real Carlie I missed. When I'd first met her I was eighteen, she'd been sixteen and free in a way I never was, but that spark seemed hidden beneath the woman she'd become. This woman would let go of my hand if I tried to hold hers right now. Just looking at the young couple made me wonder if that could've been us if we'd held on to each other.

On the fifteenth floor, the family left. Carlie pushed forward a bit so I gave her space as we rode the elevator up to the penthouse suites. So far I wasn't impressed—for the price I'd have to pay for the room, I'd expected the kinds of perks I placed in the hotels I built. I had yet to see what the Fulbright had to offer in the suite, so I reserved my judgment. Silence filled the expansive room we entered. Instead of having a seat on the set of plush sofas or going to the bedroom, I headed to the minibar and poured vodka into a shot glass.

"Do you want one?" I asked her.

"No, sir." Right down to business like always.

By the time I downed the shot and turned around, she had discarded her black blouse and leather skirt, exposing the beautiful curve of her back. The burn down my throat from the alcohol was nothing compared to the fiery need building inside of me just from watching her. Starting at her shoulders, down to the middle of her back, a bright red tattoo of a phoenix rose as if preparing for flight. The bird's wingspan spread from one shoulder to the other, and the flames cascading from the tattoo's tail left a trail for me to follow to her lovely ass. At the dip in her back, a new tattoo consisting of Latin words caught my attention—as well as the way her thighs seemed smaller.

So she really had lost weight, not much, but enough for me to notice the deeper dimple along her buttocks. As the alcohol jolted my senses, she pushed down her panties and tossed them on the couch. Every time this happened, I captured the moment in my head. The image was crystal clear. She'd walk to me like she was now and not like all the other times when she'd walked away.

When she finally looked at me, a brief exchange of messages passed between us.

Do you want me? her eyes asked as she ran a fingertip across her lips, then through her hair.

I took a step toward her. *I want to possess every part of you.*

I won't let you catch me tonight. She backed toward the bedroom. Oh heaven, I loved her tits. The dark pink tips, with their beautiful golden ring piercings, were one of her features I dreamt about the most. She was a polished packaged on the outside, but once her clothes were off, you caught her uninhibited side.

You can never escape me, I thought as I advanced faster, eventually catching her and hoisting her in my arms until her chest was pressed against mine.

For now, I had her where she belonged: with me.

Carlie

In the darkness of the suite's bedroom, I hoped Tomas wouldn't see the emotions I locked away inside of me. Every time we were together, my feelings for him welled up inside until they were overflowing.

Like when he placed me on the bed and stood over me. What I wouldn't give to stretch out the seconds into minutes. The minutes into hours.

Boldly, he waited, staring down as if he saw through me.

Did he long for me as much as I longed for him?

My fingers itched to take off his clothes so we could be skin to skin.

"What would you do if I tied you up so you could never escape me?" he asked.

I froze. "I'd still escape. I'm that good."

He closed in, and hopefully, he couldn't see the dare in my downturned eyes.

"Then I'll have to make my point." His breath warmed the side of my face, and I squeezed my eyes shut as if such an action would drive the tiger back into its cage. "You might be brave now, but when I'm done with you, you won't be sitting for a week."

I didn't dare look at his face. I belonged to him to do with as he wished. Without any clothes on, all the walls I'd built around myself were gone. If he looked closer, he'd see the eagerness in my eyes as he unbuttoned his gray shirt. My gaze drank in his hard pecs and the ink beautifully drawn on his light brown skin. From his pecs down to his hard muscled stomach, a hawk with piercing gray eyes peered back at me. Lightning bolts danced along the feathers. Among the colorful tattoos on his arms and back, that particular one had always been a personal favorite of mine. He shrugged off one sleeve then another, but he was taking too damn long.

I reached for his leather belt.

"No." His hand locked over my wrist.

I looked up at him.

He grabbed a fistful of my hair with his other hand and yanked me forward. A delicious thrill raced down my scalp as I was forced to kneel on the carpeted floor.

"Already defiant . . . Grace?" he growled.

"Patience was never a virtue of mine," I whispered.

He let go of my hair and my wrist. "Hands behind your back. Now."

"Yes, sir." I couldn't see him anymore, but the sound of him reaching into his pocket sent me spiraling into bliss. I didn't have to wait long for him to deftly cuff my hands behind my back with bondage hemp. I wiggled my fingers. I was comfortable, yet contained.

From his other pocket, he plucked out a small pair of portable shears. I held back my grin.

Safety first.

When it came to kinky sex between Tomas and me, there were only a few rules; the first being that there were no sexual boundaries between us, only boundaries of the heart. I, for one, had never been into the kinky club scene, and I suspected the same of him.

When we were together, I belonged to him. I was for his pleasure only and what he wanted to do was run a fingertip across my cheek, down my collarbone, and finally to the V between my breasts. Lower and lower his hand drifted, offering me feather-like touches over my quivering stomach until his finger brushed against my sex.

"Sir, you talk a good game," I murmured as he boldly pressed his fingertip hard against my clit. "I really —oh . . . mmmm."

"You're wet."

I was soaking wet.

"After I read your text, I've been thinking all day about touching you . . ." he said. With his other hand, he traced my lower lip. "I thought about fucking you . . ."

My mouth parted and my tongue darted out. I couldn't stop myself from sucking his long fingers, which faintly tasted like vanilla vodka, into my mouth.

He took a step away from me, tugging me to stand. Where were we going? "That mouth of yours will get you into trouble again," he whispered. "Turn around and lay on the bed."

"No." My reply was swift. I rather liked this game.

He grabbed me by the hair again and had me face-down with my ass up on the bed before I could protest. I turned my head to the side—right as he smacked my left ass cheek. Hard.

I cringed. That was just a warning shot.

He smoothed his palm over the singing skin, kneading the flesh until I almost forgot another strike would come.

"You have to control everything, don't you?" He slapped my ass twice again. The searing pain forced me to clench my fists. I couldn't bite back my cry this time. "You want to control when you come and when you go." He leaned down to draw my earlobe into his mouth as his finger slid deep inside my channel. With each stroke of his fingers, pleasure and pain blended together into a perfect melody. "But when you're here with me, I say what goes, *Coração*."

Oh, the things he did to me when he called me his heart in Portuguese. The nickname mocked my insistence to keep Carlie out of this room. Rarely, did I hear that endearment. Only behind the doors of a hotel room.

I shuddered from an oncoming climax. Tension stretched across my stomach. *I was almost there.*

Then he stopped.

I swallowed my protest, knowing what was coming.

Tomas tortured me in more ways than one.

"You ready for one more, *Coração*? That should set you straight," he whispered. I managed a nod and he withdrew from me.

At first, my body stiffened for the next smack, like it always did, but I immediately relaxed, ready and eager to take what he'd give me.

Tomas landed a solid flat palm against my right ass cheek.

"Damn it . . ." I hissed between clenched teeth. The pain was intense enough for my head to start spinning.

"That's my girl. You're lucky I didn't bring my flogger." He drew me into his arms and I melted against him. His breaths against my forehead were as ragged as mine.

Slowly, his hands ran over my arms, his touch eliciting goosebumps over my skin. The need to reach for his belt again left me trembling. I needed him inside of me—no— need wasn't right. I *had* to have him inside of me.

But saying that out loud was something I refused to do. I'd rather use actions than words.

Face-to-face, even in the semi-darkness, I couldn't think straight with his intense gaze focused on me. Our lips hovered so close together. I'd lost track of how long it had been since we'd last kissed. Years, perhaps. Now we no longer dared to do what hurt us the most, but that didn't make the yearning go away. My heart ached from the need to kiss his lips. To place my palms over his cheeks and draw his mouth to mine.

Oh, Tomas, how I've missed you.

Maybe my hands were tied for his safety as well as mine.

Tomas finally stood and removed the rest of his clothes. All I could do was lay there and watch. We'd known each other since I was sixteen and he was eighteen. Ten years had passed, yet my heart still quickened watching his beautiful naked form crawl along the bed toward me. He was the predator and I was his prey, waiting to be consumed.

I wanted him to do as he pleased and take everything I had to offer. For one night, I was willing to do that.

Chapter Three

Tomas

Seeing Carlie curled up on her side with her arms tied behind her back did something to me that was hard to describe. Strands of her blonde hair covered her cheekbones. Her full lips were parted. I loved everything about her—the way her soft green eyes followed me, the delicate flushed skin along her ass. I'd give anything to wake up with her in my bed every morning so I could fuck her again and again, but this was what I had to settle for: a night of sex until the dawn chased her away.

As tempting as it would be to sample every inch of her skin with my tongue, I knew how this game was played. I hunted and she ran.

I grabbed her legs and tugged her toward me as I knelt on the bed and leaned over her. The soft noise she made as I wrapped her legs around my hips sent the heat filling me up to a feverish pitch.

With her arms tied behind her back, I had her exactly

where I wanted her. As much as she acted like a sub, half the time I wondered if she was a switch.

Sliding into the warmth of Carlie's body, I groaned with satisfaction. Her pussy enveloped me and every errant thought I had about leaving her behind and ending this madness faded away. That's what always happened and I accepted it.

We fit perfectly together. With each pulse of my hips, she twisted hers to meet mine. At times like this, with her thighs clenching my hips and breasts brushing against my chest as she arched her back, I fell into a place where all my worries seeped away and there was nothing left but Carlie and me.

I went faster, grabbing her ass so I could go deeper. With my face settled at the crook of her neck, I sucked in her decadent pear-like scent before I sampled the skin along her neck. From there, I loved nibbling along her mouth while she panted.

"Tomas . . ."

I looked at her. Those delicious lips of hers were made to be kissed. I knew every inch of them—like how her top lip was a bit smaller than the bottom.

She moaned as our bodies met again. Our pleasure was rising again. Much faster than I'd wanted. I clenched her tighter. She urged me to go faster, her hips swirling in a manner that pushed her hard against my cock. Soon enough, she stiffened underneath me, finding her climax like she always did.

All the while, I watched, wishing I could swallow her cries with my mouth and tongue. I'd tried that the last time we met, and she'd turned her head.

Only a fool got spurned twice.

I followed her soon after; my body turning to steel

above hers. She didn't move and let me rest my chin against her forehead.

"Tomas?" She ended the silence.

"You all right?"

"Mmmm-hmm." From the corner of my eye, I caught her grin. "You seemed really relaxed."

"I am." I was at peace.

Gently, I withdrew from her and turned her over to untie her wrists. We'd done this task so many times it seemed like second nature now for me to untie her wrists and then massage the skin along her arms. First, the palms. Carlie's hands were quite small, but from experience I knew they were strong. Her wrists were always delicate, but this time I frowned at how much her wrist bones protruded.

"You look thinner," I said evenly. "Have you been working too much?"

She rolled her eyes. "I run a business—just like you— but I don't happen to have thousands of employees at my disposal."

"That's no excuse. If you need—"

Immediately, she gave me the look: lowered eyebrows, a straight line to her lips, and the dimple I adored vanishing in an instant. "I don't need anything."

She never needed anything from me until I became the last resort.

"You need to take better care of yourself, *Coração*," I said softly.

She melted a bit, taken aback.

"I know." She paused. "I've decided to change a few things while I'm back in the US. When I'm ready, we'll talk about it." She tugged me into her arms. Now that they were free, she ran her hands up and down my chest. Already, my body was responding to her bold touch.

"I plan to be a good girl," she murmured. "Right after I ride that cock."

I DIDN'T SLEEP the whole night.

Again and again, we reached for each other and gave the other what they needed, but as soon as the dawn threatened to come, I rolled over in bed and called for room service: I ordered our usual. No matter what, Carlie wasn't leaving without having breakfast with me.

She continued to slumber, snoring softly like she always did after we had sex all night. She'd always been a hard sleeper.

While she was lying on her side, I watched her naked back as she slept, the phoenix tattoo rising and falling with her deep breaths. Now that I was up close and personal I could finally read the letters on her back.

faber est suae quisque fortunae

What did that mean? I'd never seen that quote before.

I crept out of bed and hurried to the shower, taking her purse with me for insurance. By the time I got out, the food would be here and we could eat in bed like we did last time in Amsterdam.

After a nice fifteen-minute shower, I emerged from the bathroom to see her putting her shoes on.

"Going somewhere?" I held up her purse, but she snatched it back.

"Wait a sec." I reached for her again, but somehow I managed to stop myself. We were in a familiar play, and I knew the ending of this tragedy by heart.

"While you were sleeping I ordered pancakes," I said sternly. Much more sternly than I'd wanted. "With fresh strawberries."

A hint of a smile touched her lips. Did she remember how much fun we had making a mess as we fed each other? The way we died with laughter over spilled whip cream that we eventually used to sample each other's skin?

"I have important business to handle this morning," she declared.

There was always business separating us. "Of course—and when will you tell me what you couldn't tell me last night?"

"Soon. It's nothing important—I gotta make some life-style changes, that's all." She sighed, her way of changing the subject. "I'm finally looking into that address you gave me."

"So it's time to meet your birth parents?"

She nodded.

"Is there anything I can do for you?" I tugged on my pants as quickly as I could.

At the doorway, she paused. Her straight back spoke volumes. She was leaving—even if I commanded her back to my bed.

"I asked you for help, and I shouldn't have done that." Her intent was clear. "I shouldn't do that anymore. Owing you anything is a burden I'm not too good at carrying."

Owing me? So anytime I did something for her I expected something in return? Love didn't work that way. Immediately pissed off, I took a step toward her, but her hand went up to stop me.

"I really have to go, Tomas." Her face was apologetic as she made her final escape. "I'm sorry. It was great seeing you."

I clenched my fists hard enough for my fingertips to cut into my palms. Getting angry didn't change a damn thing. As usual, her final words left my heart empty and waiting to be filled again.

Chapter Four

Carlie

Leaving Tomas like that wasn't what I'd planned, but I couldn't escape that room fast enough.

I'd been awake for a while, but my eyes shot open the moment he started his room service phone call. And when he ordered the pancakes, I knew my time had run out yet again.

If I stayed, I knew what would happen. One morning would turn into a day. A day into a week. I didn't have time for heartache. Not anymore.

Any yet, I knew I hurt him. During the whole trip down the hallway, I sucked in my breaths. Anything to keep myself from crying this time or letting what happened between Tomas and me get to me. Good Lord, I should hold a master's degree in denial. I'd hang up that plaque right beside my bachelor's degree in cruelty.

Why did you text him, Carlie? I asked myself.

Because I needed to see him and feel whole again. Like four years ago.

When we were together, vanilla vodka came first. Then around three or four A.M. we'd have strawberry-covered buttermilk pancakes. And finally, before the sun rose, I'd make a run for it like a thief in the night.

No more pancakes now that I had a new diet as of a few weeks ago. *Not a new diet*, I reminded myself, *a lifestyle change.* That was what my oh-so-expensive private doctor in the UK had to say.

"Just look in the mirror, Ms. Jason," Dr. Stanger had said with little sympathy, *"the life you're living right now leads to malnourishment and pain."*

As I rode down the elevator, I tried to lift my chin higher. I was ready for change. I had to be smarter and stronger. Also, Dr. Stanger wasn't joking. Every poor judgement on my part now had a price.

Tomas immediately came to mind. *Oh, the irony.*

Two years ago, I didn't even blink when it came to eating food with gluten. Give me bread, pasta, or the like, and I'd eat it. Being picky wasn't an option growing up. I was used to cheap boxed meals with macaroni and processed meat. Hard blocks of bread you had to work hard to eat. As a kid, I ignored the minor stomachaches. There was never enough to eat, so half the time I assumed the pain was just hunger.

Little did I know I was a bomb waiting to go off.

I was finally outside the hotel and the fresh air eased the discomfort a bit. Maybe it was the space I'd put between Tomas and me.

Instead of catching a cab, I walked until I reached an intersection I didn't recognize. A bus stop bench drew my eye. It reminded me of a summer day ten years ago. On that day, the NYC weather had been milder than usual so I couldn't wait to escape my foster home with Sophie, Penny, Griffin, and my other friends. We normally roamed the streets of the Bronx, but since the heat wasn't baking us to a crisp, we took the 6 Line down to Manhattan so we could hang out in Central Park.

We usually followed the paths and people-watched. Since we never had much in terms of pocket money, we just hung out.

Except that particular day.

Penny had somehow smooth-talked her way into a grocery-bagging job, so she had a few bucks for snacks. Namely, some brain-freeze inducing snow cones. Since she supplied the cash, I was given the fun job of fetching it.

"Don't get me grape to be spiteful," Penny had said to me before I'd left.

"You'll take grape and like it, bitch," I replied. The walk to the snow cone stand and back wouldn't take me long. Less than ten minutes later I reached the intersection at Seventy-Third Street, clutching a box full of snow cones. There wasn't much in terms of traffic, but the cab drivers today seemed determined to run down anybody who ventured out into the street. While waiting for the light, I plotted on how I'd tease Penny.

"Where did you get those?" someone asked beside me. His accent was rather thick. Maybe French.

I turned to my left to see a tall guy with his hands stuffed in his wrinkled jean pockets.

He was a foreigner and I'd seen plenty of them. To visitors with cash to blow, we were just a tourist attraction.

My elbow moved to indicate back the way I came, but I paused when I saw how cute he was. You couldn't walk around NYC without bumping into a model, so I'd seen plenty of beautiful people, but this guy was gorgeous. He had the kind of blemish-free, sun-kissed skin you wanted to touch, bright brown eyes, and a smile that I couldn't help but return.

"You plan to cross the street?" he asked, his smile growing wider.

I glanced over to see the "walk" light was about to change to red.

"Shit." I'd dawdled way too long holding melting food.

"We can make it." He grabbed my snow-cone box and we sprinted across the street. I squealed as irate NYC drivers had to hit the brakes. I was breathless with laughter by the time we made the curb on the other side.

"That was so fucking stupid," I finally managed to blurt, as he handed back the snow cones. I was still smiling, even when a passing cab driver cussed at us.

Without blinking, the guy beside me yelled back in a language I didn't recognize. We started walking, and for a moment, I waited for him to walk away. He just kept on going.

"What are you doing?" I said.

He grinned and my insides turned to goo. "I'm still waiting to find out where you got those snow cones."

"Oh." I jerked my chin back the way we came. "Rich's Snow Cones. Can't miss it."

He nodded. We were still walking, and I tried to stop myself from looking down at my torn T-shirt and failed. My jean shorts weren't that nice, either.

The entrance to the park loomed ahead. I had to say something or go crazy. "What did you say to that driver?"

He shrugged. "Nothing good for a lady's ears. Especially a pretty ginger like you."

I laughed, ignoring his compliment. He thought I was a *lady*? "No, really. What did you say?"

"I said he shits out of his mouth instead of his ass."

"Hi-larious. Was that French or something?" We were almost to the park now.

"Portuguese."

I nodded. "I guess that means you're from out of town."

"You could say that, Gingerbread."

I scoffed. "Gingerbread? The name's Carlie."

He chuckled. "I rather like gingerbread."

My friends waited around a dark green park bench. I tried to think of something witty to say, but came up with nothing.

When I reached my crew, it was Griffin who noticed him first. "Who's this?"

I glanced at him and he still had that beautiful smile.

"It's Tomas," he said.

Just thinking of his carefree grin made my heart flutter. We were fools back then. Everything was simple and we fell head over heels with ease.

I finally hailed a cab. I had too much to do today to let myself sink into the past.

I had to keep moving. If I didn't, I'd head back to my room and curl up under the covers until my mistakes, both present and past, faded.

A FEW HOURS was good for the soul. I even had a salted caramel latte from Starbucks. I swear those things were confidence-in-a-cup and I felt so chipper I wanted to high-five strangers. But before I could fist-bump everyone, I had an address to visit, and I'd waited over twenty-five years for this moment. Finding Frank and Patricia Hall has been one of the most exhausting things I've ever gone through. The process began with an easy enough request five years ago to see my birth certificate. After that, my tedious search on the Internet began.

I was hopeful.

But the sheer number of folks with those names was staggering. To make things even more fun, my parents never formally got married. My birth mom merely changed her last name to match his. I got nowhere fast until I saw Tomas four years ago in Amsterdam and I vented about wanting to find them. Fast-forward to this year. A few months ago, a courier rang my bell in London and handed me a single piece of paper with an address in South Boston.

The very same address I stood in front of right now. So far, I had yet to leave the curbside and approach the single-story, white colonial home. I was finally here, but I couldn't make myself cross the patchwork front yard. The run-down appearance of the place made my heart fall a bit. Was this home the reason I was taken away? Or had my parents given me away?

I tried to shake the sinking feeling aside and forced myself to move. With increasingly sure steps, I approached the porch. Nothing would stop me from knocking on that door.

Tomas

"Good morning, Mr. Goodfellow," a security guard said with a curt nod.Since Carlie had run away, I went straight from the hotel to my workplace: the Goodfellow Tower Hotel. Might as well work to distract myself. I had tried to go back to sleep and failed. I even ate the breakfast that had been meant for us to share.

My employees gave the standard greeting as I walked into my expansive lobby. My gaze flicked from the indoor water garden to my right to the registration desk to my left.

The café connected to the lobby had a line out the door. All was well.

This was just another workday, but somehow I felt *different*.

Perhaps it was because Carlie was different this time. Usually, she opened up like a flower that only bloomed in the late summer, but this morning she'd run away as if she had something to hide.

One hour later, I sat in a full boardroom with fifteen pairs of eyes peering at me. One man in particular, with graying hair and wireframe glasses perched on his nose, stood at the head of the table.

"How many months until we can find a buyer, Kraven?" I asked, not even attempting to hide the disappointment in my voice.

Millstadt Kraven's expression never wavered. After working for the Goodfellow family for over twenty years as VP of US-based operations, he knew every intricate detail. "So far, out of the four companies who have toured our facilities, only one has expressed an interest."

Which meant no progress at all.

The Goodfellow Tower Hotel in downtown Boston was just another project. Unlike my father, who collected hotels like mistresses, I created masterpieces and then sold them at profit. Maintaining and developing new Goodfellow properties was nice and all—it was my legacy after his death—but I had no desire to add to the empire my British father valued more than my Portuguese mother. I should be grateful. Even I knew that. But when he'd abandoned me in NYC so he could chase after women and make new deals, it had left me apathetic toward the family business.

Both of my parents had been dead for a while now. All I had left was my aunts and cousins in Portugal. Once my father produced an heir with his wife, he didn't bother with having more children. My aunt Daniela tried to keep me in line from overseas, but I kept myself busy.

Three years ago, I'd begun construction on the Good-fellow Tower here in Boston. My first choice had been a site in London, but I would've only been torturing myself. Having an ocean between Carlie and I was for the best. I'd expected to be out of Boston by the time she decided to search for her parents, but she'd taken her time after my investigator delivered the information to her. She'd bought me precious time to escape.

Unfortunately, nine-figure hotel properties didn't sell as fast as they used to. Now I was stuck in Boston with her. The idea of leaving and letting Kraven handle this came to mind, but I never surrendered control like that.

Which meant I had to resist temptation—unless she came to me first. She did say she had news to share. But, then again, Carlie may never tell me. I pushed the idea of another reunion aside. She was the one who ran away from me. Knowing her, she planned to see her parents, catch up, and then jump on the next flight to the UK.

A dull throbbing hit my forehead, but I didn't move and focused on Kraven's report. Once he finished I glanced around the table. Ten folks had already mentally clocked out, perhaps hoping I wouldn't call on them. The five that were perched on their seats were new hires fresh off the line. Bates, whose receding hairline left him nothing more than a sliver of dyed black hair, appeared ready to give a riveting plan.

"Solutions?" Might as well see what my board could come up with.

Eager Bates couldn't wait to be first.

"I'm thinking we need marketing to develop focus groups. They could determine if we need to update our facilities."

"Next," I blurted.

One of the ladies leaned forward. "I'd like a thorough report on our *customer* service. Based on some initial research, our reviews have gone down a bit in the last quarter. I'd like to discuss this matter with the guest services director and the chef concierge. Are they even here today?"

Bingo. I turned to Kraven. "Where is the guest services director?"

Kraven sighed. "That's a good question."

I glanced at each face around the table. "I expect to see progress in two months or I will be reevaluating the effectiveness of this board."

One way or another, I was leaving Boston.

~

Carlie

I knocked on the rickety screen door, still giddy with excitement. Soon enough the emptiness I'd carried around all these years would be filled.

But no one answered.

So I waited, counting the cracks in the cement steps and surveying the chipped-off paint.

I pulled out my compact and checked my face for the fourth time. I looked just like I did a few minutes ago. The childhood photos I'd brought were still in my purse. Initially, I'd held them, but felt foolish. This wasn't the time to show up with a handful of baby pics while I'm flashing my pearly whites.

The right thing to do would be to smile—confirm their names—and introduce myself like I'd practiced on the plane.

Sweat gathered on my back, but I didn't move an inch from the spot in front of the door. I wanted to be here when my birth mom or dad opened the door. I wanted to be here when my parents' eyes widened seeing my face.

But no one answered.

After ten minutes, I walked around to the side and spotted a window with a gap. With a mighty heave-ho, I hoisted myself up and peered inside.

Only to immediately fall down after a brief glimpse.

There was nothing to see. The house was abandoned.

Chapter Five

Carlie

I wasn't sure how long I sat on the porch. Maybe too long for the policeman who drove by twice. On his third lap around the block, he gave me the look. I didn't exactly look like I belonged.

I frowned the whole *damn* time and I was a bit over-dressed.

Before I came I had these expectations, the whole house would've smelled like breakfast. That was what I always imagined. Buttermilk pancakes and warm oatmeal for the first course—I always imagined my birth parents were rich by the way—then another course of biscuits, bacon, and ham cut up in small bite-sized pieces.

But the house was empty, clearly uninhabited. I'd taken a cab to get here, but now that I didn't have anything to show for my trip, I began to walk. Might as well save my money.

According to my smartphone, I had a good five blocks to the nearest subway entrance. Not too bad.

I should've worn running shoes and some comfortable clothes, but I'd wanted to look nice. I'd pictured myself hugging my mom wearing my best bright blue coat. She'd compliment me on the Hermès heels I'd hiked here in.

My cellphone dinged. *Did you meet them?*

I cringed from Tomas's text message. Why did he have to ask? After years of silence between us, our time together last night still made my skin tingle with pleasure. I even craved the burn on my backside.

Walking through this neighborhood was bittersweet. I passed a playground and immediately wondered what it would've been like if this school had been mine. Would I have played here with friends? Would the woman I am now be different? Not that I didn't love the lifelong friends I'd made in foster care, but in my fantasies, I imagined that there was something special about childhood friends who grew up knowing each other's parents. I was just another kid who sat around waiting to be adopted. Folks would come visit my foster home and I'd smile, trying to arrange my unruly curls and wipe away freckles that had no intention of hiding.

What got me every time was my mouth. Where others were quiet and soft-spoken, I was the bold girl who outright asked people where they lived and if they had a better place than the foster home.

This particular neighborhood with its single-story colonials and fenced-in yards, wasn't perfect by any means. Signs of graffiti and overgrown grass peppered things here and there, but families had barbecue grills and swing sets, and probably celebrated birthdays and good times together.

What I wouldn't give to have experienced that kind of stuff.

By the time I managed to reach the subway entrance,

my feet were killing me. The trip on the Silver Line back downtown was uneventful. Almost deathly silent.

What are you gonna do now, Carlie?

Good question. I had no leads and I had no plans to connect with Tomas again. Just seeing that empty house was hard enough. My whole body throbbed at the thought of seeing him. The easy thing to do would be to text him back and tell him my parents weren't there, but that opened doors I didn't want opened. Tomas and I were like that. I could still taste the liquor on his lips, smell the spicy cologne on his chest. If I closed my eyes, I could feel his pulse thrumming against my fingertips. Feel the harsh grip of his hands on my hips while he thrust into me again and again.

My thighs clenched with need, and I bit my lower lip. Being with Tomas always complicated things.

What if you really made an effort this time? I always asked myself.

I held back a laugh. We'd both tried that and failed. When two career-driven people are forced into a relationship and have no interest in being tied down, one of them will walk away—and most likely leave the other person bitter and closed off.

THE MONTH PASSED MUCH FASTER than I expected. Twenty-four hours before I had to exit stage left from my hotel, I took stock of what I had on my king-sized bed: fifteen pairs of shoes, ten designer dresses, enough lingerie to open a boutique, and two pairs of jeans. I *really* had my priorities straight. My fingers ran over the delicate lace of my dark red La Perla bras. Growing up, I couldn't afford lingerie like this. Time and time again, while looking for work around Manhattan, I'd pass stores and peer inside at the pretty clothes. I had no doubt that someday I'd get what I wanted. I just had to be willing to work ten times harder than everyone else.

Now I had to let this proof of my success go to keep searching. I still had a return ticket to London sitting in my purse, but I wasn't ready to cash that in yet. I'd sacrificed so much to come here—money, control of my business, everything I'd worked for was on hold. And I needed cash.

Let them go, Carlie, I reminded myself. *They are just things.*

I opened my Michael Kors carry-on bag and started stuffing dresses and shoes inside. I already had a few upscale resale shops in mind. Might as well tear off the Band-Aid and put on my big girl panties.

After a phone call to update the temp I'd hired to run my business in London, I ventured out. Three trips later, I had enough cash for a few weeks at an extended stay hotel for business travelers in north Boston. It wasn't the suite I'd been living in. I didn't have room service or a massive tub. Back in the day, I used to wash up in a gas station bathroom. At this point, I was grateful to have a roof over my head.

Now that I had a new home, I didn't sit on my ass though. I checked many places, from the Suffolk County property records to the Veterans Benefits Administration. None of them had any information for Frank or Patricia Hill either. Go figure.

As days passed, my money supply slowly went down. *Which meant it was time for me to hustle.*

Compared to a few of my affluent customers in the UK, I wasn't afraid of hard work. Matter of fact, I thrived on it. Asking my friends in the area for help was out of the question so I checked my sources to see if anyone in my network needed an assistant for a brief period of time. A few phone calls led to nothing.

"As much as I'd love to work with you, dear, I'd need you out in California," one said. Or they'd say Seattle or New York City, or some other location that wasn't Boston. I was hungry for work, but I'd pushed off finding my parents for too long.

Now was the time.

So I did what anyone would do when they had run out of options. I went to a temp agency. I was usually the one finding work for other people, but sometimes you gotta go find the folks who need workers. I might wear Louboutin heels once in a while, but I was never above working as a cashier, an administrative assistant, or things like that. I'd met too many debutantes with their attitudes stuck so far up their asses they wouldn't survive a nuclear winter if their butler ran away.

So I went to the temp center.

The interview didn't exactly go as planned.

"So I see on your resume you own a concierge company in the United Kingdom. How nice." The young lady behind the desk, who appeared to be about fifteen going on sixteen, peered at my paperwork.

I nodded and smiled. You should always smile. "Miss Fields, I can do anything from event planning to finance management, or errands for clients."

"I see." Miss Fields's bright orange cardigan made me squint a bit as she adjusted her red and green glasses. "We don't have anything in event planning, but we've had a position that keeps re-opening that might fit your needs."

A position that is never filled? That was never good.

"What do you mean?" I asked.

She shrugged as if it was nothing. "Oh, the last temp said something about her boss being *crazy,* but I see this as a great opportunity to jump in as an assistant to someone who oversees fifty employees."

I kept nodding. *And smiling.*

She continued. "With a resume like yours, you seem like that someone who'd tackle the job with ease. You know, take the bull by the horns."

Of course. *The crazy bull by the horns.*

"I'll see if I can get you an interview and we'll go from there," she chirped.

Three hours later, I had a phone call and an address. Now that was fast. I had to catch the bus now since I wasn't downtown anymore and taxis were out of my budget. The trip was nice.

With a spring in my step, and my last pair of Louboutins on, I bounded up to the building.

I was right outside a recent construction: the Good-fellow Tower Hotel.

ON ANY OTHER DAY, I would've marched right in there so I could kick some ass at the interview, but like a fool I imitated a tree on the front steps.

You need cash, Carlie. Have you ever let a man get in the way of your hustle?

Never, I told myself firmly.

I took a step forward.

What if you see him?

I wanted to smack the shit of out myself for thinking that.

If you see him, you ignore him. We had one night together. We got a quick screw out of our system and he was doing his thing and I was doing mine. *Like we always do.*

I was closer to the building this time. With each step, I told myself I wasn't going to fold like I had in the past.

For all I knew, he was probably out of the country. He was an international hotelier and, at this moment, he was probably living it up with some snow bunnies on a slope in Switzerland. Tomas rarely hung around after we hooked up.

I'd never been here before, but if the hotel looked this amazing on the outside, the inside had to be gorgeous. Three massive letters in gold, GTH, sat in a fountain in the front. All of this was a testament to Tomas's wealth. You couldn't be a businessman without knowing the Good-fellows.

And I had an interview here.

After speaking with someone at the concierge desk, I took the elevator up to the second floor. As the doors snapped shut, my heart fluttered. Would I run into him?

I was filled with relief when I reached a quiet floor filled with dark-blue cubicles and modern desks. Plants peppered the corners. This was just another hotel business floor for management. I left the elevator and walked up to the receptionist desk.

"Are you Carlie?" the receptionist asked softly.

"That's me."

"You must be the new victim. I'm Stephanie."

Hint number two that this place was gonna swallow me whole.

"Welcome to the Goodfellow Tower Hotel," Stephanie said. "Let me take you to Roland Butts. He's the chef concierge and oversees the customer relations department for our premier clientele."

"Is that my supervisor's name?"

"Yep, and I wouldn't get it wrong if I were you," she whispered. *"Ever."*

Stephanie led me down the corridor between the desks toward a closed-off office. The only one in the room. The leather chair for Mr. Butts's assistant sat empty and the desk had a layer of dust thick enough to resemble a blanket of snow. Not a good sign.

The door to his office was closed, so Stephanie knocked softly. I barely heard a mumble from within and then the receptionist entered with me on her heels.

While the desk outside this room appeared abandoned, this room was well lived-in. From one side of the narrow room to the next, the walls were covered with built-in bookcases. None of them held casual reading materials, either. A quick glance revealed cookbooks, protocols for foreign countries, even books on basket weaving in the Maldives. My gaze flicked to the tall, bearded man sitting behind the immaculate desk. The pale gentleman wore a perfectly pressed navy blazer, along with a Hermès handkerchief tucked into the pocket. The guy sat straight enough to make me question my posture.

"Would you like a fresh coffee, Mr. Butts?" Stephanie asked softly.

He glanced up from his Mac computer monitor. His perfectly manicured short fingernails were typing away. "I could've used a refill *ten* minutes ago. I got my own."

Stephanie's smile faltered.

I stepped forward and extended my hand to end the awkward moment. "Hi, nice to meet you."

Instead of shaking my hand, he said, "Thank you, Miss Gaines. You may leave now."

He turned to me the moment she hightailed it out of there. "I think we should make things clear from the get-go so there aren't any misunderstandings."

I tried to keep looking at his face, but the way his hands hovered over the keyboard as if he was in the middle of a thought and planned to continue typing unnerved me. Wasn't I here for an interview?

Mr. Butts continued. "I expect perfection. I work with exclusive clientele and every single person who was hired to assist me was unable to tell their rear end from their mouth."

Nice. He wasn't a bullshitter. Now this was an employer I could get behind.

He typed again for a moment, clicked the enter key, and then dabbed some lotion on his hands. Without looking, he placed the silver bottle in the *exact* spot he'd picked it up from.

This guy was no joke.

Since this was such a high-end hotel, I expected Mr. Butts to be very professional, but then again, if I oversaw a place like this I wouldn't have any room for burnt ends. It had been a while since I'd worked in a hotel, but the quality of the staff was all in the hands of the management. Piss poor management equated staff reading their cellphones instead of handling customer problems.

He stood and I waited until he moved toward the door. "Just because you've worked in both the US and the UK, doesn't mean you'd know how I expect things to be done at the Goodfellow."

"Yes, sir."

"I'm not your *sir*," he said crisply.

I meant no disrespect, but I knew how to hold my tongue. "My apologies, Mr. Butts."

He opened his door and I swiftly followed. *We're moving, people.* "On your resume, I noticed you're not fluent in any foreign languages."

Now that was one strike against me. Unlike my best friend Sophie, who also owned a personal concierge business here in Boston and spoke fluent Japanese, I hadn't mastered any foreign languages. I had rudimentary skills.

"I can greet and help customers in Spanish, French, and Portuguese. I'm not fluent by any means, but I'm more than capable. I'm quite familiar with the interpreters available in the Boston area."

He walked faster. "Most of our clientele is from Europe, but every now and then we have businessmen from Asia and Africa."

I nodded, paying careful attention to every word.

The elevator doors closed behind us and I held my breath. My ears always painfully popped, no matter what I did.

"Do you know American Sign Language?" he asked.

"I am proficient in fingerspelling." My head hurt a bit from nodding so much. "I've assisted blind and deaf customers before."

In my previous interviews, there'd been no tour of the facilities until I had the job, but it looked like Mr. Butts was offering me one. Hope filled me and buoyed me upward. I kept smiling, hoping and praying we didn't pass Tomas.

"Mr. Goodfellow believes our customers' privacy is of the utmost importance," Mr. Butts said. "Ever since the Tower opened last year, we've had a policy in place to insure everything that takes place in our hotel is private."

I nodded, yet again. If he only knew the secrets I'd kept in the past while I'd worked in the big cities, the blond hairs on his head would go white. The madness ranged from week-long parties with foreign call girls to ushering elderly gentlemen to the hospital because they took a few too many purple pills to keep their peter in action.

It was simple in my opinion. I had a job to do and I did it—as long as I didn't endanger myself or others. After Mr. Butts showed me around the customer service floor, he gave me a full tour of the hotel. The whole place seemed brand new, but with the classic charm of Boston in the 1920s.

Not long after the tour ended, I stood waiting for his verdict.

Mr. Butts looked me over, perhaps searching for a flaw. "I'm interested in working with you because of your membership in Les Clefs d'Or, Ms. Jason, but only on a trial basis. I have thirty-five souls as concierge staff for the premier clients at the Goodfellow. Just because you've worked with high-class clients in the UK, doesn't mean you have the skill set to work in a hotel again."

As he spoke, with the utmost confidence I'd fail—I forced myself to keep a straight face. I'd been working full-time for the past six years in the service industry and he thought I might've forgotten a thing or two? At least my membership in the elite Les Clefs d'Or hotel concierge organization showed merit.

"I have full control over hiring the assistant chef concierge and I expect all my clients to have the utmost care. I'd prefer someone who spoke at least five languages, but . . ." He looked me over, maybe expecting me to flinch, but I didn't.

"Are you up to the challenge?" he finished.

"Yes, Mr. Butts." The only direction was up, right?

He turned to enter the elevator, but stopped before I could get on. "Then I'll see you bright and early at six a.m. Tomorrow."

Chapter Six

Carlie

Fogginess dulled my brain as I tried to tug off sleep. And failed utterly. One day I was going to wake up on time. Three alarm clocks beeped, sang, and chirped respectively. My fourth alarm, one with the annoying shrill of a tornado siren at full blast, vibrated the whole bed.

At least something worked.

Without an alarm, I rarely got up on time. Except when I woke up in Tomas's bed, but that was a place I couldn't wait to escape.

In five minutes, I was dressed in the standard staff uniform for the Goodfellow Tower Hotel: dark blue pencil skirt—right above the knee—a white blouse, and a black blazer with a golden GTH stitched into the front pocket.

Right before I'd left the building, I'd picked up my clothes and signed the employment forms at the security desk.

The stack of papers I had to sign included a lengthy

nondisclosure agreement. I'd seen plenty of these in my line of work, so the legalese wasn't a surprise, but the consequences of breaking the agreement bordered on extreme.

I signed and let it go. If Tomas's company was willing to pay me well to keep secrets, so be it. The sooner I found my parents, the sooner I could return overseas and get back to running my own business.

Not long after getting ready, I took the subway with the rest of the commuters. North Boston around the Cambridge campus wasn't too bad. Everyone around me looked about my age with a few older and younger commuters sprinkled here and there, but most of them were likely mid-twenties graduate students on track to teach or work research jobs after they escaped college. As we reached downtown, I took in each face, from the short girl wearing scrubs to the bearded man who dictated into his phone, and imagined their lives were my own. In another life, I'd attended a four-year college, and now I worked for a living.

In my imaginary world, on weekends, I called my parents and they complained about how I never made time for them. A smile touched my lips. I was busy taking over the world, after all.

That was the life I'd lived for the past few years and now no matter how much I focused on each step toward the Goodfellow Tower Hotel, I was still Carlie Jason, orphan, hermit, and the girl who wanted this emptiness inside me to fade.

My step quickened. Entering the hotel at the staff entrance, I was excited about the possibilities. I was on the front lines again and I might learn a thing or two.

The last thing I expected was to find a Hispanic couple arguing in the hallway the minute I reached the service level. The man, who had an enormous brown stain across his shirt, silently fumed while the woman across from him tried to argue in hushed tones.

"Is there anything you can do right?" she snapped. "It's your third day and you've already stained your clothes."

I kept my gaze forward.

She continued. "Just turn around and go home."

"No one will notice." Even though he was a bit shorter than the woman, he appeared to be quite resolute to take the punishment and not argue about what happened. Were they married?

"No one will notice? How about the coffee smell?" she hissed.

Oh, I noticed it. Starbucks Mocha Latte with Vanilla and Cream. Joy in a cup. I shouldn't drink it anymore, but if I could, I'd pump the creamy, caffeine-filled goodness into my veins.

I almost walked past them. If I helped I'd be late, but then again I wasn't the kind of person to just stand there and let fate Hulk-smash someone's job into the ground.

"Hey." Both of them turned toward me. I got the look I've seen countless times in NYC. A single raised eyebrow, head tilted to the side and downward turn to the mouth: namely mind-your-own-business lady.

"Just trying to offer a hand here." I saw the name Yolanda on her name badge. "Yolanda, most departments have backup clothes."

"Like they are going to let us use them for free."

"We're working in a hotel. Accidents like spills are going to happen." I took a step closer. I had their attention now.

"So what do we do?" she asked.

I smiled. "Follow me."

They had to rush to keep up; I didn't want to be too late.

"Harry, c'mon!" Yolanda said.

"Who is your supervisor?" I asked.

Yolanda fired off a name I didn't recognize, but I'd learn everyone's name soon enough. I knew exactly where to go. Last night I'd gone over the materials I asked for from security: the map of the entire facility, the services the hotel offered, and nearby restaurants. All of this was my arsenal.

And I fired a pretty bad ass gun.

In record time, we reached the laundry services floor which was right next to dry cleaning services. The whole place was impressive. Instead of placing the dry cleaning services in a corner, Tomas had devoted an entire space to dry cleaning. I scanned the room, noting the state-of-the-art garment press and washing machines. *Not bad, Goodfellow.*

I quickly found the backup uniforms among the shelves of folded clothes and grabbed what I needed.

"Can I help you?" one of the maids asked.

"Harry needs another shirt. He had a mishap on the way in. A patron spilled her latte on him." I grinned. "I'm Carlie Jason. I'm working with Mr. Butts."

The ladies around us laughed. "So you're the new victim," one of them said.

Should I be concerned everyone thinks that? "I'll be fine."

Once I left laundry services, I found the couple in the bathroom. They were still arguing.

I handed the shirt to Harry. "Once you're done with it, turn it in. It's that easy."

"How did you know his size?" Yolanda glanced from me to Harry, who shrugged while he donned the fresh shirt.

I laughed. "My job is to take care of people, Yolanda. When it comes to customers you have to not only read what they want but also read them as people. Your husband probably weighs one hundred eighty pounds and has a thirty-four-inch waist. His neck tends to lean on the thick side at eighteen inches, but a shirt around seventeen and a half should fit him just fine."

They stared at me as if I'd stripped down naked.

"You're good," Harry remarked.

"Are you for real?" she asked. "What's your name?"

I introduced myself. "You can't get any more real than me, sister." I glanced at my watch. Four minutes left. I might make it on time. *Might.* "I gotta go. See you two around."

I hurried out of the there and ran to the service elevator. They managed to join me before the door shut.

"Thanks, Carlie," Yolanda mumbled.

"You're more than welcome." I smiled and finally she grinned back. Yolanda was rather pretty when she wasn't chewing poor Harry out.

By the time I stumbled into the management offices on the second floor, I was only three minutes late. Not bad, but for my new boss that wasn't so good.

First things first, I used a tissue to wipe off a spot for my purse. That was when I noticed the open door to Mr. Butts's office. I peered around the corner and didn't see anyone sitting at the desk.

I got into the seat with a contented sigh—only to see him standing with his arms crossed on the other side of the room.

Shit.

"Good morning, Ms. Jason," he said tersely.

Hearing my name forced me to stand. "Good morning." My voice was somewhat forceful.

Mr. Butts snorted. "Glad you could make a *strong* impression on your first day."

Saving the world had its pitfalls. He picked up a tablet and marched out of his office. I hurried to keep up with him.

"We have a lot of business to conduct today," he began. "A few fires to put out and I need to show you the twenty-second floor."

I frowned, recalling how the twenty-second floor wasn't on the map I memorized. "What's on the twenty-second floor? We don't have a thirteenth, which is standard, but a missing twenty-second floor is rather—"

"At least you've been studying," he said crisply. "Mr. Goodfellow invested over one hundred million dollars into this property to bring opulence to the Boston area. The Tower has high profile customers, and it's our job to make sure our guests on the twenty-second floor are comfortable."

We weaved around the service floor past the cubicles and the conference rooms. A business meeting paused for a moment as he passed, as if they were waiting to see if he'd enter.

"I thought I was supposed to assist you with any concierge management problems?"

"Yes, but primarily I need someone handling the sensitive issues I don't have time to handle."

As the chef concierge, Mr. Butts saw everything. The concierge was for anyone to use, but like me, Mr. Butts handled the big fish. I was prepared for anything though. From organizing a garden party for rich wannabe blue bloods to sending businessmen from overseas on a fishing trip in the Atlantic, this was just another day.

Mr. Butts continued. "Your paperwork has been processed and everything is in the clear."

He hovered the keycard in his pocket over the reader in the elevator. A green light flashed on the opaque white button. "Your new keycard gives you access to the twenty-second floor." He demonstrated. "Hold your keycard over the reader for four seconds and wait for the flash. After the flash, you'll be taken to the twenty-second floor."

Apparently, that was the only way to get there. I didn't see a button for the twenty-second floor.

On the way up, the car briefly stopped to let staff in and out. Each of them nodded to Mr. Butts. On the way, I pondered where we were going. Did the Tower have an exclusive concierge floor? I'd seen plenty of those before as well. Those places put most resorts to shame with butlers for massive suites, personal master chefs, along with any desire fulfilled.

Mr. Butts turned to me. "In your packet, you signed a nondisclosure agreement to never allow other staff members on this floor."

I nodded.

The doors slid open and a man entered the elevator. "Good morning, Roland."

I froze upon hearing that silky voice. He always had a way of turning my insides to liquid.

Even on my first day I couldn't escape him.

Tomas had found me.

Chapter Seven

Carlie

"Is this your newest employee?" Tomas asked. Like always, he was perfect at showing the world what he wanted them to see. The face that had hovered over mine while he was inside me now smiled as he greeted a subordinate. Stiff, yet friendly.

I wanted to take a step back, but resolve made me stand in place. *Don't let him see he has affected you*, I thought.

"This is Ms. Jason's first day," Butts said. "I'm taking her to the twenty-second floor."

"Of course."

I forced myself to stand closer to him.

"Can I help you, sir?" Butts asked in Portuguese.

I swallowed, understanding that much. Hearing Butts call him "sir" bothered me for some reason. Maybe it was the endearment I sensed behind his statement. Roland respected him.

Tomas replied in English. "I thought it'd be important

to give your assistant a tour myself since the twenty-second floor is very important to many of our guests."

Butts nodded. He turned to me and stood with a straighter back. *Don't make me look bad,* was what his expression said.

I couldn't help looking from Tomas's wide back down to the way his black slacks fit over the curve of his ass. Damn he was a perfect specimen. He was taller than most men, and it was apparent in how Butts had to look up at his employer.

Finally, we reached our destination. With an audible ding, the door opened. Tomas stepped through first, leaving a haze of his cologne behind. For a moment, I wanted to stay behind in the elevator and let his scent course through me.

Instead of staying though, I followed Butts out onto a long hallway with marble floors. Tomas stepped aside so Butts could take the lead. We followed him, words still lingering in the air between us, until we reached the end of the hallway and paradise unfolded.

I slowed a bit, unable to keep up while taking in everything around me, from the marble floors covered with gold and vermillion rugs that extended toward grand staircases to the expansive ceilings with elaborate white wainscoting. Excruciating detail had been taken to carve the Goodfellow coat of arms on the white walls.

We'd stepped from a modern hotel to a section better suited for royalty. My smile froze in place the moment I saw a brunette crawling along the red carpet on her hands and knees. A deep purple leash ran from a collar around her neck to a short man's gloved hand. The sway of her bare hips and small breasts was hypnotic. The dark-haired woman didn't have a bit of clothing on and her gaze was set on the path before her.

"Are you taking Millicent for a walk?" Tomas asked the man.

"Just a quick jaunt," the short man said. He wore casual business attire. Almost as if he'd just left work for the day.

Briefly, I glanced at the man Tomas had spoken to, only to look away for a moment. The short man's light brown eyes were intense and he smiled at me with appreciation. "Who is this exquisite creature, Mr. Butts?"

My boss piped in. "Mr. Frasier, Ms. Jason will be assisting me from now on."

Tomas angled a bit in front of me and, for a brief moment, a flicker of possession sparked in his eyes. "She's here to accommodate all your needs, but she's not available to sample."

"How unfortunate." Mr. Frasier quirked a grin. He dangled his right hand at his side and Millicent angled upward, eagerly trying to stroke her cheek against his palm. My mouth dried just watching the way her lips parted and her breasts pressed together as she reached. What I wouldn't give to be in the same position at Tomas's feet. Eager and wet to service him.

"I'm in the middle of showing her Dante's Second Floor," Tomas said. "Please enjoy yourself and let the staff know if there is anything they can do for you."

So this was place was called Dante's Second Floor.

Now that was an interesting name. Even I caught the reference to the Italian masterpiece *The Divine Comedy*. In the poem, Dante descended into hell, passing through nine circles. In the second one, he encountered people guilty of lust.

With a nod, Mr. Butts continued walking and I hurried after him. I told myself not to look back where Tomas spoke quietly with Frasier, but I glanced briefly behind my back to see them looking in my direction.

At Frasier's feet, Millicent stared at me too, a delightful grin on her perfect, red mouth.

From the hallway, we walked down a stairwell toward an open room with a massive Grecian bath. I spied two pools, along with a seating area with chairs and tables. Four hot tubs were filled with guests relaxing and talking.

Mr. Butts extended his hand toward the room as if he was giving a casual tour. "Please note the layout, Ms. Jason. This floor doesn't have a map available to the public. Concierge, guest services, and a cleaning staff are available twenty-four hours a day. If you notice anything that isn't meeting Mr. Goodfellow's expectations, you have full authority to act."

Somehow, my supervisor was all business while a couple no more than twenty feet away from us fucked.

While Mr. Butts pointed out where I'd find supplies such as bath oils from Dubai and pure wool towels from Scotland, I tried to ignore the rising heat in my body. The woman moaned and I could practically feel each thrust as if the guest was fucking me. Then he withdrew and parted her legs. I knew what was coming and tried not to stare, but with a brief glance I saw him bending over to suck at her clit.

I'd seen sex in kinky clubs before, but I'd never been serious about the club scene. If I wanted pleasure and pain, I preferred the moment to be private with a partner. But, I was human, and hearing her little moans and the wet sounds of sucking made my thighs clench with need. I could see Tomas bending down in front of me, his eyes dark and his tongue stretched out to run from my inner thighs into my wet channel.

"What do you think of the baths?" Tomas's voice entered my din and I had to quickly switch gears.

"Absolutely opulent," I began.

Mr. Butts had left my side to examine a cart with toppled over items in one corner. He quickly gestured for a staff member to clean it up.

"That's not what you're really thinking." Tomas's voice was like a caress I hungered for.

Honesty was something we always tried to have between us. If one person wanted to leave, we both accepted it, but at this moment, I didn't want to reveal my longing. We weren't alone.

"You didn't spare any expense here," I said. "Your efforts are impressive."

He nodded. "There's more."

"Of course, there is. I'd expect nothing less than the best from Tomas Goodfellow." He was good at so *many* things.

Not far from us, the delicious cries of the woman's climax rocketed through me. I wanted to be that woman. Immediately, the man turned her over, pushed her ass in the air, and slid inside of her with a single thrust. The sounds of their flesh meeting forced me to turn away from Tomas before I said or did something I'd regret.

Not far from the baths, Mr. Butts led us to a grand hall. In the middle of the room sat larger tables where guests ate lunch or had drinks. Most of the guests were naked or close to it.

A woman, dressed in tight black leather from her neck to her heels, was flanked by two naked men, while at another table, a man was down on his knees drawing another man's cock into his mouth.

This place was a kinky playground for the rich.

"No wonder you have such stringent rules for an assistant," I finally said to Butts.

He rolled his eyes. "I expect perfection, but I will admit, the last assistant I had took one step in here and walked right back out. We have select clientele, and if you have any qualms about the business conducted here, I don't have time for shenanigans."

I laughed a bit. He had no idea . . .

"Mr. Goodfellow assured me, after he learned you'd been hired, that you would be a perfect employee and you'd accommodate our guests' needs as a professional."

So Tomas knew I was here before I'd even stepped through the door. Not good.

"Do you have any objections?" Mr. Butts asked.

"Just another day at the office," I chirped. We circled the outside of the room. All the while, Mr. Butts checked the tables and made sure the servers were keeping up with the customers. My gaze swept over the space as well. There was more than enough waitstaff. The food swiftly came out of the double doors to the far right and the servers carried the trays with expertise.

Whenever someone dropped something, another staff member quickly swept in to retrieve it.

I noticed Butts had left my side so I caught back up with him and realized Tomas was gone. I searched the room, but he'd disappeared.

"Let's go, Ms. Jason," Mr. Butts said. "We have more to see."

He wasn't kidding. There was a room for every type of carnal desire. We passed a library where a naked, thin man browsed books. Another room with a theater stage where a woman played a concert piano in nothing more than a single ribbon tied to her hair.

"The gentleman looking for books is Mr. Marston Ericson," Mr. Butts supplied. "He owns stock in one of the biggest investment firms in the Northeast. He is *particular* about our services. We had to install storm doors in the library so he could read in absolute silence. Apparently, noise from the outside is unacceptable, but if you've got a couple making *merriment* a few feet away he doesn't mind."

I swallowed a laugh. Butts had yet to say anything crass. With all the *merriment* going on around him, he'd have to use metaphors for everything.

This place was getting more interesting by the minute.

Mr. Butts's phone in his back pocket went off. He sighed and read the screen. "I need to end this tour. We've got an irate guest in the Darkness Suite and security has been called."

"I can manage it."

"No, finish going down that hallway." He pointed where I needed to go. "Familiarize yourself with every room, except the Darkness Suite, until you reach the end." Butts was somehow furiously typing on his smartphone while feeding me these instructions. "Loop back around until you reach the service elevator you started from."

I nodded.

"This floor will keep you more than occupied," he threw over his shoulder as he left.

More than occupied, huh? I didn't know if that was a good or bad thing.

I walked through one glamorous room after another. In one room, there was nothing on the walls but mirrors. Right now, the space was empty, and beautiful golden couches with brocade fabric sat without guests. Instead of continuing down the hallway, I entered the room. What stood out were three beautiful mirrors that ran from the twenty-foot high ceiling to the floor. The rest of the mirrors were smaller and thinner and wrapped along the wall. As I approached, my heels clicking on the floor, I spotted a reflection behind mine. My breath caught to see Tomas.

I wanted to say something, but for once I was without words. I looked over the mirrors to distract myself. Perhaps there'd be a smudge or something for me to wipe, but the room was immaculate. I ran my fingers along the carved wood framing on one of the massive mirrors.

He was closer now, a shadow warming my back.

Don't let him affect you, Carlie. But it was too late. We were standing too close together again and I could taste his cologne on my tongue. My body quivered from the memory.

"You won't find any flaws in my mirrors." His gaze swept over me and I wanted to turn around but couldn't.

I looked at his beautiful face from his chin to the perfect curve of his nose. He still had the same tiny scar from childhood. The warmth in his brown eyes darkened and my insides melted. A single chocolate brown curl strayed from the others on his head. There weren't any other flaws in the reflection I saw. He was perfect in my eyes and that was why my feet inched toward the right. If I kept going, I could finish looking over the room and leave as if I hadn't considered temptation.

"They're perfect," I managed to say.

He was closer now. I took another step to the right.

I waited for him to touch me, but he didn't. "You shouldn't have come here, Carlie," he breathed.

The resonance in his voice was like a melody my body wanted to sway to.

"I needed a job."

"You could have worked anywhere. You're very good at what you do."

I resisted touching the mirror. My face grew flushed

with heat and my lips parted.

I waited for him to take a step forward and mold himself onto my backside.

But he didn't budge. We weren't hooking up in a hotel room right now.

The temptation to look in his eyes was almost overwhelming. I could see everything else, but I refused to look at his face anymore.

"I can't stop looking at your lips, Carlie." His whisper was an invitation. "Ever since that night, I can't stop thinking about you. Or those lips you won't kiss me with."

We had kissed before, though. Many years ago when we'd gone so deep down the rabbit hole neither of us wanted to escape, but when life came crashing in to pull us apart, we came to an unspoken agreement.

Satisfy, but don't get too close.

My heart lurched at the thought. The last time our lips had touched was eight years ago. The pain deepened.

This isn't the place, Carlie.

I never fucked in the same place I worked. What Tomas and I did was private. Keeping things private was the only way to separate fantasy from reality.

And at the moment, reality told me being alone with Tomas wasn't wise.

He approached me until I couldn't escape.

~

Tomas

All I was supposed to do was give her a tour. Sounded simple enough when I saw her arrive this morning, but now that I had her pinned in front of me, I wanted nothing more than to possess her again.

I stepped over the line we used to separate ourselves, but I didn't care. Her blonde hair was beautiful and thick, practically beckoning me to grab a fistful and pull her head back to expose her graceful neck. More thoughts came to mind—like pulling up her skirt, and entering her from behind.

Which meant my appetite hadn't been sated yet . . .

Wanting Carlie was nothing new. Our brief meetings always satisfied me for a while, but now that she was close, my control was withering away. I ran my hands down her sides until I found the hem of her skirt. My fingers played with the hem, then gripped it hard.

The words "bend over," sat on my tongue, and my breath quickened.

If you asked her, she'd surrender to you.

But her surrender wouldn't be what I truly wanted. I forced myself to add distance between us. I wanted her to turn around and put her arms around me. I wanted to see the joyous light in her eyes when we were together outside the bedroom. Carlie could be cold without working hard at it. Ever since that first day we'd met back in NYC when she was sixteen, she always had something to say. Her feelings weren't something she held back if she was hungry, cold, or wanted to have fun. But her heart was another matter.

Please turn around, Carlie.

She didn't so I took another step back.

"Do you have any questions about this floor?" I asked her.

"Not at the moment, but I'm sure if I have any, I can ask Mr. Butts."

Of course, she'd ask him. She only came to me for one thing.

"I'll leave you to that then."

Chapter Eight

Carlie

One week into working at the Goodfellow Tower Hotel, and my search to find my birth mother wasn't going well—but I had high hopes. My list had *nineteen* women named Patricia Hall, who, over the past twenty years, had lived in the Boston area. Apparently, Patricia Hall was a very common name. The run-down house was the only record I found for Frank Hall, too.

If that wasn't enough fun for me, I felt lost every time I ventured onto the twenty-second floor. And every couple was a reminder of my relationship I kept behind closed doors.

Most mornings, when my shift began, I toured the floor to take care of any customer needs, but the sheer vastness of this place left me at a disadvantage.

And then there were the clients.

From one corner to another, I encountered the most fascinating people. I kept seeing one particular guest every time I delivered white orchids to a young Japanese couple who ate their breakfast naked. He seemed to prefer the table *right* across from them.

This particular day, after I placed the massive boutique on their table, the man called out to me, "Hey, Jason."

I stopped mid-step. "Are you talking to me?"

"It's Jason, right?"

I held back a laugh. My name badge read Carlie Jason. I didn't remember Jason being first. I walked up to him. Now that I was up close, I could appreciate how pretty he was. Not that pretty was bad—but it wasn't my type. As I approached him, I took in the smooth perfection of his light brown skin and high cheekbones. Bluish-gray eyes focused on my face instead of my legs. Which was rather refreshing. His lips were full, practically made for kissing. Compared to most of the other men in business suits, this guest wore blue jeans that were torn in the knees and a red flannel shirt. Yep, the dude was rocking flannel on a hotel floor where rooms cost over a grand per night.

"How about *Ms.* Jason?" I asked.

He feigned displeasure. "I like the way Jason sounds. Calling someone *Ms.* feels pretentious, doesn't it?"

"Not necessarily. Can I get you anything?" I didn't have time to get hit on by someone who had been scoping me out long enough to know my name.

"Isn't the customer always right?"

"No."

He laughed.

I was smiling now, too. He relaxed against his seat and picked up a glass with a green slush-like juice.

"Can I get you a fresh"—I took a closer look—"whatever that is...?"

"It's fresh kale, spinach, and cucumbers. And a bunch of healthy shit I can't identify." He frowned at the half-empty glass. "Want some?"

I wasn't tempted at all. Any minute now the sludge might start moving. "I'll pass. You don't want to finish it?"

"I'd rather have a lobotomy—after I eat a stack of waffles and with a side of bacon."

He had good taste. "You and me both."

"Have a seat then, Jason. Take a load off for a little while."

"Thanks for the offer, but by the time I prop up my feet, someone will set something on fire or I'll have another mishap to deal with."

He nodded and took a sip of his water instead. The juiced veggies were probably sentient and ready to topple the Tower by now. Our attention was diverted as we watched Mr. Frasier lead a leashed Millicent to one of the tables. It was just like any other day for them. Millicent curled up her long legs under the table.

My outspoken patron openly stared. "I will admit, Jason, you look like you don't belong here." He wasn't looking at me anymore, even when I glanced at him.

"And what's that supposed to mean?"

He shrugged. "Every now and then, you always have this far away look on your face."

I swallowed, wondering when he'd seen me like that. Had he caught me thinking of Tomas?

"Your boss Roland has the *focus* of a surgeon—but you're a lot more relaxed. I like that." He quirked a smile and my stomach warmed at how gorgeous he was. He probably had no trouble finding a partner on this floor to play with.

I sighed. Time to end our conversation before things got too personal. "I'll try to liven things up then. Wouldn't want you to get too comfortable with your mystery drink, *mister*?"

"Carver. My name's Carver."

Now I had a name to a face. "Have a good day, *Mr.* Carver."

He rolled his eyes. "Murphy is my last name—and nobody calls me Mr. Murphy except Roland."

I nodded. While I walked throughout the room, and not once did Carver move from his spot. Only his drink shifted. He pushed the awful green stuff farther away from his water.

I ordered him a brand-new one before I left the floor.

Chapter Nine

Carlie

A s far as I could tell, most of the guests who stayed on this floor seemed to live here. I didn't see too many new arrivals over time.

Over the past couple of days, I'd explored all the rooms, except for one. I'd yet to enter the Darkness Suite.

You may assist customers in every room except for the Darkness Suite, Mr. Butts had instructed me a week ago.

Not many people went inside. There were two signs outside the door. The first sign was ornate and burgundy-colored. The script was whimsical as if written by hand: *You have come to a place mute of all light, where the wind bellows as the sea does in a tempest. This is the realm where the lustful spend eternity.*

I smiled. This was Dante's description of hell's second circle. So far I'd floated through the light-filled clouds on this floor, and yet, the room in front of me promised something much more than darkness.

The second sign was much more straightforward: *Space*

for scene play is available on a first-come, first-served basis. Only trained Doms may enter after a background check.

Good policy. In the past, I'd never expected myself to fall into the BDSM lifestyle. Tomas had been my introduction over eight years ago. We were young then and foolish, but time passed, and that one particular summer when everything seemed to fall apart for Sophie and me with a pending eviction notice, Tomas had been there for me.

In more ways than one.

Now there weren't many kinky pleasures I hadn't experienced. For me it was about finding the next thrill. My defiant nature had gotten me into trouble quite often. Meeting Tomas in hotel rooms made it hard for us to act out scenes.

So why hadn't we met here instead?

I approached the closed door. The sweet scent of vanilla lingered nearby. Why didn't Butts want me in here? Was the order from Tomas?

I glanced around. Seeing that I was alone, I opened the door and ventured inside. A quick peek wouldn't hurt.

Spotlights in the center of the space revealed bondage tables, benches, and even a Saint Andrew's Cross. Only blue lights along the floor illuminated the edges of the room. Shadows sucked in everything else. Unfamiliar faces dotted the corners. Five men and three women watched a scene unfold in the center of the room. A curvy brunette with short, cropped hair leaned over a sawhorse. Even from where I stood on the other side of the room, I could make out the dimples along flushed ass cheeks. The fresh welts, as well.

One man lightly caressed her right ass cheek with a riding crop while the other two watched in silence.

The need to see more pushed me forward.

No one said a thing while I lurked in my dark corner.

The stark sound of the crop striking her flesh made my lips part. I still distinctly remembered the night I'd lost my virginity to Tomas.

Get on my bed, Carlie, he'd said to me that night. Every single word still affected me.

Instead of being tied to a sawhorse, I'd been tied to his bed. Just remembering the tension in my limbs left me heady.

The crop struck her flesh again, and she moaned.

I wanted to moan, too. Before I'd lain on his bed, Tomas had touched me until I was begging. His fingers fluttered over the sensitive skin of my stomach. He caressed my collarbone and nibbled the skin along the underside of my breasts. All the while, he avoided the throbbing place between my legs. When I was trembling uncontrollably, he ordered me to his bed.

There's something I've always wanted to do to you, he whispered. *Ever since I met you, I've wanted to possess you. Both in body and spirit.*

I wanted to give him everything. All my secrets. All my passions. Surprisingly, all the guys I'd dated since Tomas had been pretty good, but none of them had come close to driving me crazy with want.

The man approached the woman on the sawhorse and bent down to bring her nipple into his mouth. He sucked hard and my core clenched from the way his tongue curled over her flesh. He ran his hands down her hips, his caresses reverent and gentle. With deft fingers he slid his index finger inside of her.

My knees buckled a bit, watching her reaction.

You should go, Carlie. There's a reason your supervisor didn't want you here.

But I couldn't move from my spot.

Time passed as she rocked back and forth on his hand.

Ecstasy filled her features and I couldn't resist floating away with her. Her back arched, and every sensation she felt flooded my body with remembrance: Tomas inside of me. Tomas's mouth on me.

The man whispered encouragement to her until she sagged against her bonds. Sated and pleased, he gently unstrapped her. Now that the scene had ended, the group shared a conversation or two before they left.

I slid deeper into the corner, making sure they didn't see me. Something bumped my leg. In the darkness, I couldn't see what I'd hit. I peered into the shadows and my mouth dropped to see armchairs along the wall. In the seat I bumped, a man sat cross-legged.

"What are you doing here, Ms. Jason?" Tomas whispered.

Tomas

Hunger manifests itself in us in many ways. Whether we hunger for love, food, shelter, or sex, we search endlessly to sate our innate desires. For me, that hunger was often lust. That growing need to possess what I couldn't have cut through me. Again and again. I'd found the only way to quench my thirst without Carlie was to come to this room and watch.

On occasion, I brought other women here, too. I'd strapped them to the table and pleasured them until they panted under my eager hands.

But none of them were Carlie.

For me, longing replaced lust.

Seeing her in my personal domain brought back the ache I tried to shove away. While the scene played out, she thought I hadn't seen her hiding there, but I had. My body ached just watching the way she sagged against the wall.

"What are you doing here?" I asked again.

Her mouth moved. In the darkness, I missed seeing the deep flush along her skin or the way she bit her bottom lip when she was turned on.

My hand snaked out and took her arm. She didn't fight me when I drew her into my lap. "I'll ask you one more time."

"Working." A mere whisper I strained to hear.

"This room doesn't need supervision. Didn't Roland tell you?" In my lap, her body molded to mine. My grip on her wrist tightened. Her pear scent enveloped me, urging me to draw her closer.

"You were watching," I said.

"Yes," she admitted.

"Why?"

"You know damn well why." She clammed up.

"It's amusing to have you speechless for once."

She snorted.

I sighed. "I've missed you, Carlie. I want you to stay with me tonight." The words were out of my mouth before I had a chance to stop myself.

She sat there, sucking in deep breaths as if she were considering what I'd said. I waited for her to get up, but she turned around and hiked up her skirt up to straddle the seat. "You need to stop feeling that way..."

When I didn't answer, she reached up to run her palms down the sides of my face. She traced along my chin and drew a single fingertip over the bridge of my nose to my lips. I shuddered from the light touch. Instinctively, I opened my mouth to suck her finger in, but she pulled back with a pout.

"Don't tease me..." I grated out.

That damn mouth of hers would be the end of me. I did miss her. Day after day, even as I tried to distract myself with another construction project, she was on my mind. My hands moved of their own volition and did the same thing she'd done to me. Except I ran my thumb along the seam of her mouth. She sucked my thumb into her mouth and the velvety warmth of her tongue sent shocks of pleasure across my stomach.

Heat flared in her eyes. I'd seen this expression before. She was about to take what she wanted. Ever so slowly, she slid off my lap until she rested on her knees and her hands lingered on my cock, now straining against my pants.

There was no discussion as she freed my length.

Stop her before this goes too far. But any thoughts of leaving the room faded as she drew the tip into her mouth. Heat surged up my shaft and I closed my eyes. I'd asked her not to tease me, and of course, she disobeyed. It was always about my pleasure, but on *her* terms.

"Owing you anything is a burden I'm not too good at carrying," she had said to me.

Stroke after stroke of her hand sent me spiraling deeper toward a place only she could take me. There was something about the way she looked up at me with worship in her gaze. I closed my eyes and imagined she was the old Carlie again. She had her curly red hair again, a sprinkle of freckles across her cheekbones, and a devilish dimple near her wicked grin.

I wanted to tell her how much she pleased me, how I couldn't get enough of her, but my mouth refused to open. This would be another scene between us, and like a fool, I'd admitted I missed her. As she brought me closer to climax, I almost wanted to push her away, but she was relentless until I groaned and shuddered, gripping the armrest hard enough to my fingers to go numb.

Then it was just the two of us in a silent room. Nothing resolved. Only lust sated. And now Carlie was my employee.

She tried to rise, but I grabbed her wrist. "Don't leave yet. We need to talk. You told me you had news to share."

"This isn't a good time. Maybe over coffee sometime," she whispered, blind to what I really wanted from her: *her love*. "Someone might come in here," she added.

"As if you'd ask me out for coffee. Let them come. My name is on the door."

She sighed and glared at me briefly. I refused to let go. "We can't keep doing this to each other. Every night I think about you and I wonder what would happen if we just had a normal night together."

"What we have isn't *normal*, Tomas."

"Why can't we try normal?" No more meet and fuck. "This isn't like that week in New York."

Now that made her pause. Mentioning what happened to us eight years ago wasn't wise, but we were at this point for a reason.

"You know how the story ends," she said. "What happened eight years ago will happen again: You *will* walk away. You *will* let your business control your life. And in the end, you *will* leave me standing there trying to figure out what's left of myself."

"Don't you think I might have felt the same when I had to go back to college?"

I felt like a recording playing on repeat. We'd had this conversation many times before.

"We've been fuck buddies for a long time," she said, her voice tired.

"We're more than that."

"Do you honestly believe we can change?" Her voice began to rise. "So far, your track record doesn't look too good, either. First, it was boarding school every summer—which I hated, but accepted. Then, after I fell in love with you when you were in college, you didn't bother to say goodbye after you jaunted off to Europe—"

"Don't—" I let go of her. My dad had just passed away and at the time, I didn't want to burden her with my anger. In hindsight, I should've taken her with me back to Europe, but exposing her to the sharks swimming after my father's fortune wasn't something I'd *ever* let happen.

"Don't do what?" she said quietly, biting her lower lip. "Don't *hold* on to us? To protect myself, I had to learn how to let you go a long time ago."

With that, I got up and left before I'd say something I'd regret. At least, this time I was the one leaving her behind.

Chapter Ten

Tomas

I *shouldn't have left Carlie like that.*

That single thought circled my mind all after-noon into the evening, even as Kraven discussed figures at our business dinner after work. The restaurant near the marina had the best cod and the wine flowed, but I couldn't enjoy the food.

Ever since I walked away from Carlie a few hours earlier, that week she mentioned weighed heavily on my mind.

While Kraven spoke about changing seasons and the decrease in guest visits since the summer was winding down, a particular summer in New York City eight years ago came to mind. A fog of humidity had blanketed the city making anyone who ventured between buildings miser-able. Those first six days, nine hours, and seven minutes had changed my life, and it all began with a phone call.

After the standard, "Hey, it's Carlie," and my moment of surprise, she went on and on about how she'd plucked my number from a crumpled up piece of paper in her winter coat and thought about calling me. At the beginning of the summer I was always the one who reached out to her when I got back in town from college. Ever since we'd met two years ago near Central Park, she'd known my phone number, but this was the first time she'd called me.

This was just another game she played. She acted as if this was a casual call, and of course, I canceled any plans I had to immediately pick her up. After we met up though, and found a small cafe to eat lunch, she grew quiet, even scraping her food around her plate.

"What's on your mind?" I'd asked her. "You usually eat like you're preparing for war."

She wrinkled her nose, an endearing sight with all that red, curly hair framing her pretty face. "Sophie and I have our own place now."

"Sounds good."

More food pushing. Her grip on her fork tightened. "We're going to be evicted unless we come up with the rent money." She swallowed deeply. "I need . . . help."

She refused to look at me, delving into the facts: they had no money or anything of value to sell. When we spent time together, she never asked for help or a handout. When I had money in my pocket, I paid for things.

The desire to tell her she didn't need to justify her request sat on my tongue, but for Carlie, actions spoke louder than words. I immediately picked up my phone and made arrangements with my bank to send the money to Sophie so their rent would be paid up for the next year.

That was the last time Carlie asked me for anything.

With the matter settled, we didn't bring it up again. Now that I was back home from my third year at Oxford, I wanted to enjoy my time off. To distract her, we visited our favorite places around NYC—with air-conditioning. After that, we never left the penthouse. Spending time with Carlie was easy like that. I didn't have to think about my business studies, my Portuguese aunts' expectations, or the obligations of a Goodfellow heir. It was about the time we spent, not the money spent.

As we fell deeper and deeper in love in the span of a few days, we discussed the things any couple naturally did: how she'd come with me to the UK. How we'd make a life for ourselves instead of stealing time every summer.

Five days into the week, I'd even bought her a promise ring.

After we'd had sex that night, she rested her head on my chest while I played with her hair. Finding an opening to give her the ring eluded me so I left the box under my pillow.

"I just wanted to say thanks," she said out of the blue.

I sighed. "You don't need to."

"Yes. I do." She turned over until she faced me with a smile. "It took Sophie and I months to save up money for that place. We did it *all* on our own. I just can't tell you the high I get every time I accomplish something on my own."

She kissed my shoulder. "I will pay you back. Every cent."

I tapped her dimple. "With interest?"

"Don't push it, Goodfellow."

Lying naked with our limbs intertwined, we snuggled under the covers and fell asleep—until an insistent knock on the door drew me away. Carlie didn't stir as I left the bed, donned a robe, and found my butler, Saul, waiting at the door.

"I'm sorry to bother you, Mr. Goodfellow," he began, "but there's a phone call you must answer."

My stomach tightened. Since I was a kid, Saul had called me Tommy. Never Mr. Goodfellow.

I took the phone call in the study.

"Your father is dead, Tomas." My aunt Lucia's empty voice filled the line.

Instead of dropping into the seat, my fist clenched. Out of all the people to call, I wanted this news from Aunt Daniela. My mother had three sisters, and only one of them really gave a damn about me. The Pereiras were a respectable, affluent family in Lisbon, but their wealth was dwarfed by the Goodfellow empire.

"You need to be in London as soon as possible, before your father's mistresses smell the blood in the water," she implored. "Those damn *putas* aren't getting—"

"How did he die?" Right now I didn't feel like hearing her diatribe. She'd always been bitter that my father neglected my mother. Even worse when he didn't continue to support my aunts financially.

She was quiet for a moment. "A heart attack. Although, I wondered if he had a heart in the first place. You need to be concerned about your legacy." She paused again. "As well as our villa in Porto."

My hand tightened around the phone hard enough to hurt.

My father is dead and now I'm the heir to the Goodfellow fortune. Why worry about the sharks in the UK when one had found me already?

"Where's Aunt Daniela?" I asked.

"She's on her way to the airport. She'll be here in a few hours."

Which meant Aunt Lucia was already in London.

"I'll be there soon," I said after a long released breath.

"Good, good." Afterward, the brief moment of silence felt awkward. This was where normal people would've said something to comfort the other, but I got *nothing*.

"Goodbye, Aunt Lucia."

After the call ended, I sat there for the longest time, unsure what to do. The logical thing would be to wake up Carlie and get on a plane, but that was the easy way out.

We'd made plans—now none of that meant a damn thing. I'd have to stay in London for who knew how long. Carlie had a life here. There was also no way in fucking hell I was exposing her to Aunt Lucia and the rest of the women who planned to assemble and bicker over a dead man's fortune. That night in the study, I formed a plan: settle this mess and then come back for her. I got dressed and left Carlie a note that I had business to handle.

But I didn't return for over a year.

And now, eight years later, I was eating dinner with Kraven and not Carlie. I never gave her that promise ring, either. I was preparing to sell my hotel and move onto the next location and the next project.

Her words bounced around my head: *You walk away and leave me standing there trying to figure out what's left of myself.*

Yes, I had done that.

And I'd give anything to go back to that day so I could've stayed instead of leaving. For that day, I did the very thing that hurt her the most.

I'd abandoned her.

A FEW DAYS LATER, my mood was buoyed. The second meeting with the team from Hong Kong was going better than expected. If everything proceeded as planned, I'd not only have a buyer for the Goodfellow Tower but I might have a partner to provide an ideal location for the additional property I was looking at.

"We're seriously considering your fine property, Mr. Goodfellow," the lead from the team in Hong Kong said. I scanned their eager faces, assessing their interest based on their reactions. So far, so good.

This was just another meeting and another set of potential buyers, but as my gaze swept over the meeting room on the conference floor, the tension in my stomach increased a bit. Of all the hotels I'd constructed, this one in Boston was special.

So why are you selling it? I asked myself.

Because this was just another property.

No matter how many extra touches I put into the building or how much I worked on the façade, this was only another multi-million-dollar investment that would pay off in the end. *Remember your goals,* I reminded myself.

Since I was a kid, I'd dreamed of an ideal project. A place where I could do what I wanted to whomever I pleased. I created such a place as a whim here in Boston. The goal though had always been to go bigger and higher.

I wanted the kind of investment property that could only be dreamt of and then brought to life through an architect's drawing. In my mind, my resort would have beaches, entertainment spaces, and luxury shopping spaces.

I thought my next project would be Dubai or London, yet, I ended up in Boston, even contemplating going back to NYC again.

I couldn't help smiling. *You always come back to the US because this place is where it all began.* Maybe someday I knew she'd come back. If not for me, then for something else.

After the preliminary presentation, where I was all smiles and such, Kraven began the tour. Usually, I sat back and waited for them to finish the process, but I couldn't resist going along this time.

I told myself it wasn't to see if I ran into her again. I had no desire to see the fiery look in her eyes after what happened between us, but one glimpse today would be enough to recharge me.

During the whole tour, she hadn't showed up once.

My heartbeat sped up thinking about the moment we stole in the Darkness Suite. She'd been responsive like she always was, but the moment I expressed how I felt, she played her withdrawal act like a professional.

I sucked in a deep breath. I shouldn't have asked her to stay with me last night, but I did it anyway. As much as she liked to receive pain, I got a healthy dose of it myself.

The tour ended and I had yet to see her again. Today I would have to settle for the memory of our time together.

"So what are your initial thoughts, Mr. Phuong?" I asked my guest.

"Based on my assistant's reports you have made a sizable investment in the construction. The architectural details are phenomenal. May I ask why you're even considering selling this property?" His expression was sincere, but this was what all of them asked. Why put so much love in and then let it go?

I asked myself that question often. "This is what I do. I'm passionate about creating properties, not maintaining them. A piece of me went into every part of this facility. I'm ready for the next challenge. Wherever that maybe."

Chapter Eleven

Carlie

Going for a walk with my boss, Mr. Butts, was closer to torture than productive work. The inspections, as Mr. Butts called them, were nothing more than him looking over my shoulder on a weekly basis. As meticulous as I was though, Roland Butts took things to the next level. When I browsed conference rooms for any trash or chairs out of place, he was on the floor looking for *absolutely* anything.

In the past I'd had all sorts of employers. The glassy-eyed ones were the worst. One summer I worked at a Brooklyn hair salon and half the time I wondered if the lady doing the weaves was even awake. She'd stare into space while sewing in hair the wrong way. Of course, later I learned she was up all night watching telenovelas on the local Spanish channel.

Now I had a keen-eyed barracuda who patrolled the waters for a fresh kill and I was about to be served up today.

Maybe his keen eye was the reason I got caught staring at Tomas while he spoke with a group of Asian businessmen in the lobby.

"*Ms.* Jason . . ." Mr. Butts's sharp comment caught my attention and sent me scampering after him. By the time we got to the Grecian baths on Dante's Second Floor, his proverbial feathers were ruffled as I checked the pools. He also had yet to let me know if I was still working on a trial basis or if I actually had a job. "I have concerns, Ms. Jason."

"May I ask—" I began.

"I mean I have concerns about your *relationship* with Mr. Goodfellow."

That made me stop short. He whispered the word "relationship" as if he'd said a bad word.

"Let's get something straight here." Lying wasn't something I wanted or needed to do at this point. "I did have a prior relationship with Mr. Goodfellow, but that was a long time ago. Way back before I'd even left for the UK. We don't fit together well. You may perceive something between us, but I see it as him irking me half of the time."

Butts casually rearranged perfectly placed towels while he berated me. "I have a strict policy about employees fraternizing with the executives. It creates issues with nepotism."

"Nepotism?" I picked up a tiny balled-up piece of paper someone left on the floor. "The guy is selling your workplace to the highest bidder. He has no interest in me. He's interested in passing you and me off to someone else." I knew very well what that group of businessmen was here for.

"Who owns the hotel doesn't matter, Ms. Jason. For all you know, we could be heading toward higher pay and better benefits."

I wanted to laugh so hard it hurt.

"Have you ever worked overseas in a hotel, Mr. Butts?"

Now that made him stop. "No, I haven't had the opportunity."

"Try working for a company in Asia or Europe before you say ownership isn't irrelevant. It's a different game over there. We may have to provide the same level of service to our American customers, but the corporate structure will be different. For all you know, this kinky floor is going bye-bye if a conservative company buys the hotel."

Butts sighed. "A fine idea actually . . . A guest asked me to order *butt* plugs the other day.

"*Mr.* Butts, have housekeeping bring more towels and some *butt* plugs, please," he grumbled in a singsong voice.

I swallowed a laugh and tried to keep going on the subject at hand. "Employees' insurance benefits will change, and possibly not for the better."

Mr. Butts sighed. "Whether or not the new owners make changes doesn't matter in the end."

"True."

If you're smart, Carlie, you'll uncover your parents and get out of here before you do something with Tomas that you'll regret. No more hotel drama, no more Tomas, just making money in London where I want to be. Where I have a life.

An ocean between us would put me back on track definitely.

Later that afternoon, I spotted Carver sitting in his usual spot by the pool.

"Hey, Jason!" he called out.

He always made me smile. I placed a fresh, green smoothie next to his old one. His smile faded. "How are you, Carver?"

"Feeling good. Two hot models just made out on the other side of the pool."

This man is too much. The guy was attractive enough to have at least a few models hanging all over him, but as usual, he was sitting by himself.

"Should I get you some binoculars?" I asked.

"Naw." He took a long drink from the fresh glass. "My vision is perfect . . . when I watch my sugar anyway."

"Do you have diabetes?"

"Yeah, I got Type II." He chuckled. "I'm not the most compliant patient either, according to my doc."

"Don't feel bad. I'm not, either."

"What you got?"

I picked up his old drink and considered the door I'd just opened. Talking to Carver was too easy. Discussing my personal business with guests wasn't wise, but just looking at him relaxed against his seat, not a single line of stress on his face, set me at ease.

"I have celiac disease and I'm not dealing with it well . . ."

He briefly threw a smile my way. "Is that the disease where you can't eat things like wheat?"

"Pretty much. I'd kill for a cheap bottle of beer right about now with a huge plate of deep dish lasagna."

"Aren't there gluten-free options now? You don't have much to complain about. Have you tried sugar-free apple pie?" He shook his head as if disgusted. "It's like a culinary murder scene during my family dinners. My aunt makes this *a-mazing* brown sugar, baked sweet potato dish that everyone loves and I'm the knucklehead stuck eating a plain baked potato."

"It could be worse."

"How?"

"You could be allergic to potatoes."

He rolled his eyes. "Does your family cook something different for you?"

I shrugged. "I'm an orphan."

"Damn, I'm sorry."

"Don't be. I have friends who I consider my family . . . and I'm here in Boston to find my biological parents." There I go again, but talking like this feels good. It was like I was hanging out with Griffin. Both of them were fine as hell and they had an easy nature about them.

He slowly nodded. "How's the search going?"

"I have a feeling I have a better chance finding you a *tasty* piece of sugar-free apple pie in our kitchen than finding my parents."

He grunted. "Have you ever tasted sugar-free apple pie before? Thanks, but no thanks. Even at my company meetings they serve me that shit."

"Company meetings? I've yet to see you do *any* work."

"That's what underlings are for. I got a bunch of managers."

With an amused grin, I watched him tilt his head to better observe Millicent as she went by with Mr. Frasier. Their timing was flawless.

"What kind of company do you own?" I asked.

"A private investigation firm out of the Midwest."

"Sounds pretty cool."

"How come you haven't hired an investigator to find your parents?"

I shrugged again. "No money. Even I know how much you guys cost."

He gave me the kind of smile that would melt the iciest of hearts. "What if you had a good friend who gave you the home girl hook up?"

I made a face. "I'd thank them, but I'd have to decline their offer. I'm doing pretty well on my own."

One of his eyebrows went up. "How long have you been looking?"

"Not long . . ." The muscle in my cheek twitched with the beginnings of irritation. His offer seemed sincere, but I didn't want to owe a new friend—let alone a hotel guest— such a huge debt.

Maybe he read the doubt in my expression since he was quiet for a bit, but he wasn't quiet for too long. "You might not want my help, but the least you could do is hook a brother up with a *real* smoothie every once in a while."

I snorted. "I don't mind being your apple pie supplier, but I'll feel guilty after I have to call the paramedics when your blood sugar spikes."

"See, Jason! That's what I like about you." He winked at me, his gray-blue eyes glittering with mischief. "Always thinking ahead."

How I wished thinking ahead solved all my problems. Especially those involving Tomas.

Chapter Twelve

Tomas

The meeting with the prospective buyers from Canada went well, but they hadn't expressed as much interest as the company from Beijing. Every property had a rhythm, its own vibe. I had to find buyers who connected with my work. Their lack of interest didn't make my work day any easier. I'd been looking for a distraction. It was always about her. Having her so close to me, only a few floors separating us, made this day all the more difficult to manage.

Today was Carlie's birthday. September 3.

Her birthday had never been an event we celebrated. The day came and went when we were apart. We'd never been together during her birthday. Matter of fact, the last time we'd spent an extended amount of time together, she'd left me behind one week before her birthday.

Each year her birthday appeared on my calendar, though. She was always in the back of my mind, but today she was front and center. I glanced at my calendar—which was always full—and considered what needed to be done to clear my evening.

I called in my assistant Wendy. "Any chance we can cancel my dinner meeting with my board?"

"You have a last minute meeting?" she asked, immediately pulling out a notebook and pen.

"Not exactly. I need you to run a few errands for me." The smile on my face grew wider. "Today is going to be a good day."

~

Carlie

Today sucked. It could only get better, right?

"Stop being a grumpy bitch," Penny quipped during a brief phone call I had with her over my lunchtime. "I spent half the afternoon searching for the best spot for tonight. We can't wait to surprise you."

"With strippers dressed as firemen?"

"Puh-lease. I'm not a *miracle* worker."

I sucked in a silent breath. After I moved to London, I always spent my birthday alone in a private spa. I got the full treatment. Five hours of massages and facials left me gooey with absolute bliss. Hanging out with Penny meant I would be trying weird shit all night.

"Make sure they have gluten-free options," I added.

"Of course."

Last night I told the crew, over a group text, about my lovely doctor visit. I kept things nonchalant and, as expected, they did the same. That was why I loved them. I still had to tell Tomas though—he'd want to know.

Penny continued. "I'm spending my money, hard-earned by turning virtual tricks, to get you the best tonight.

One of my customers said you will absolutely *die* from how divine the food is."

I fought back a smile. Maybe some time with my best friends would be just as good as frolicking at the spa. Penny worked hard for her money as an at-home phone sex operator and she wanted to show me a good time.

"I've got a few surprises up my sleeve, too," she added.

As we ended the call, my smile faltered. I was finally celebrating my birthday again with my family. I hadn't found my parents yet, but at least I wouldn't be alone. Even if Tomas wouldn't be there.

As I finished my lunch, an egg salad with a perfectly prepared gluten-free English muffin, I looked forward to evening's events. Hanging out with the crew was rarely dull. We would either sit around and nothing would happen or shit went down. If I was a betting gal, I believe tomfoolery was guaranteed with Penny in charge.

Two hours later I was back on Dante's Second Floor checking on hotel guests, when my personal cellphone rang showing a number I didn't recognize. None of my customers knew the number so I picked up.

"Is this Carlie?" a deep voice, drenched in Southern charm, drawled.

Huh? "Yes, it is. Who am I speaking to?"

"This is Bill."

I slowed down on my way to the pool room. "Bill . . . who?"

"I'm a friend of Penny's. She wanted me to call you to make sure you had a *pleasurable* afternoon. An afternoon delight, so to speak."

"Excuse me?" I squeaked.

"She told me you like to be spanked."

What the fuck? I was in the middle of checking the pool room and one of Penny's oddball phone sex customers was calling me as if I wanted to hear this shit right now? Well, two can play at this game.

"Give me a sec, Bill. I need to go to a private place."

"Of course!"

With a grin, I put the phone on mute and I walked over to a table of familiar guests and placed the phone in the middle. The three models were on vacation from the UK. So far they hadn't done much this morning other than sipping their drinks and relaxing.

"I'm getting pranked," I explained. "Who wants in?"

All three women nodded with interest. I'd picked the perfect crowd who wanted to play.

Free guest entertainment, anyone?

I turned off mute.

"Hey Bill, I'm back. Can we role-play?" I asked.

"Hell, yeah, darlin'." His deep voice was smooth. "Would you like it over my knee or maybe I should strap you onto my bed?"

"I love to do different voices," I purred. "Can I do that for you, too?"

"Mmmm-hmmm."

A blonde girl at the table stifled a giggle.

I gestured for one of them to speak.

"Knee please. I've been so fucking naughty today," the blonde quipped. The brunette across from her clamped a hand over her mouth to keep from laughing.

My work here is done.

I left my new friend Bill behind to do some work. Naturally, a small crowd gathered around the phone.

While I was working with the other concierge staff in the Grecian bath to make sure all the guests were comfortable, Bill apparently had no idea he'd just spanked most of the women who lounged around the pool.

When I went back to fetch my phone, the blonde and

the brunette were perched over the phone as Bill panted. "Oh baby, you like it like that, don't you?"

Another slap filled the air from the phone. *Who the hell was he spanking?* Hopefully not his junk.

By the time Bill, the king of spanking, climaxed, I picked up the phone and turned off speaker system. "Wow, Bill, you're amazing."

"Not as amazing as you. Damn, you're talented."

"I'm waiting for Hollywood to call me, baby."

Today was going much better than I'd expected.

The afternoon ended with a bouquet of balloons and flowers from Sophie. Penny left a gift box at the main concierge desk containing a pair of bright red, crotchless panties. The note in the box said: *Pretty panties for pretty bitches. Use wisely.*

How eloquent of her. *Well played, Penny.*

I could've come up with something raunchier though.

I usually only had one phone call a day from my best friends, but today was shaping up to be quite interesting. Not a single gift or message from Tomas.

Maybe he was too busy with selling this building to care. I shouldn't mind, though. We'd never celebrated each other's birthdays. Tomas was a New Year's baby. At least a bunch of people partied during his birthday.

The only folks who celebrated with me were the souls celebrating Flag Day in Australia.

My heart clenched—even though I told myself I didn't give a damn. I shouldn't expect anything other than what we already did every year.

Absolute silence.

∽

Tomas

The plan was simple. Also rather brilliant, if I do say so myself.

Carlie's shift ended at five p.m. sharp and she never left early. According to Butts, she always checked the five concierge desks on Dante's Second Floor before she ended her work day.

So why was it five-thirty and the lady in question had yet to make an appearance?

"Would you like for me to call the concierge desk?" my driver asked from limo's the front seat.

I was parked in front of the employee entrance, waiting in a car full of balloons, along with a bouquet of vibrant yellow and lavender dahlias—Carlie's favorite.

Ten minutes later, I gave in and called the concierge desk.

The explanation from the front desk was quite the eye-opener.

"Ms. Jason got several gifts today. It was her birthday apparently. An Indian woman dropped off a box—she seemed so excited about taking Carlie out to eat."

That had to be Penny. "Did she mention where they might be going?"

"A name wasn't mentioned, but when she said Carlie was going to love the raw squid they planned to throw at her, I was able to narrow it down."

Only a few places in town served raw squid, and soon enough I'd be there.

Chapter Thirteen

Carlie

"For someone as laid back as you are, it was hard as hell to get you to leave work early," Penny grumbled to me.

I tried to get a bit more elbow room since I was squished between Penny and Sophie in the backseat of the cab. "I happen to *value* my job compared to some people who have random customers call their friends."

"How was Bill?" she purred. Her eyebrows danced with mischief.

"He spanks like the best of them," I replied, remembering the grins on the models' faces.

"Boy, do I know," Sophie murmured.

"What do you mean?" I asked.

I couldn't help smiling at her. The blush in her cheeks spoke volumes.

"Let's just say I will never fill in for Penny," Sophie said as she pushed her dark hair behind her ear. *"Ever."*

I laughed until my side hurt and Penny joined me.

"Did one of her customers drive you to say your safe-word?" I joked. "I gotta know."

Penny winked at me. "Bill says he's willing to pay extra to get some of Shelley again."

"*Shelley?* Is that your phone sex girl name, Ashley?" I asked. "Why not Diamond or Candy?"

"*Bitch,*" Sophie mumbled with a smile. She hated when I used her birth name—especially since her full name was Ashley Sophie Ashton—but I only teased her with love.

The opening melody to a popular Black Eyed Peas song came on the cab's radio.

"Turn it up, please!" I yelled.

Without missing a beat, all three of us sang the opening to "My Humps" at the top of our lungs.

This song brought back good memories. Whether we could sing or not didn't matter—it was all about the fact we were together again. Penny strutted her stuff while Sophie was so off-key it was painful.

Once the song was over we were breathless but smiling. I leaned over to speak to Sophie.

"So how's it going with Xavier?" I said in her ear. Since the beginning of the spring, Sophie had been dating Xavier Quinn, a hotshot technology mogul from the southwest.

"Great, he's in Thailand doing business for his family." She pursed her lips as if displeased. "I might see him before the fall's over so we can plan our wedding next spring."

Penny laughed. "Why can't you just elope?"

"The Quinn family has to invite every relative west of the Mississippi. When you got old California money, everyone and their second cousin are invited."

"As long as you're together, that's all that matters." We continued to sing our favorites on the way to the restaurant. I was glad for the distraction, though. Over and over again I told myself this day would end well—even if I only had my family to celebrate with.

Soon we pulled up to a trendy sushi place. I had to watch out for my nemesis, soy sauce, but otherwise I'd be fine. And I loved, loved sushi. In my opinion, rainbow rolls should be a food group.

"I can't wait to show you what I ordered for us," Penny gushed. "I ordered ahead to make sure everything would be safe and such."

"And what would that be?"

"You'll find out." She stuck her tongue out at me. "What fun would it be if we had boring food?"

Fine. I'd let her have her fun today, too. My mouth was practically watering. The moment we walked in, I tasted the cucumbers, fish, and rice on a California roll.

Since Penny had reserved our seats, we didn't have to wait long to be seated in a massive booth in the back. As I glanced from face to face, a sense of happiness settled over me. Griffin was here and he got up briefly to hug me. With creamy, light brown skin and hazel eyes, he was just as cute as he was as a kid. Back when we were younger, his face was fuller—a bit pudgy if anyone asked—but now he had the kind of sharp angles in his face that were guaranteed to break a few hearts.

To his right, Sophie picked up the menu, even though Penny had said she'd pre-ordered, and she had a far away look in her light blue eyes. Maybe it was the new fiancé in her life that made her seem so self-assured.

And then there was my partner in crime, Penny. Boy, had she changed. She was just as much of a loudmouth as she had been in the past, but I never expected one of my best friends to become so drop-dead gorgeous. I'd give my next paycheck to have her cheekbones and straight, black hair. (Even though it was blonde now…) The other day I'd even teased her about looking like the Bollywood actress Aishwarya Rai Bachchan.

Penny tried to snatch the menu from Sophie, but Sophie leaned out of the way with practiced ease. "I know you. I'm not eating fugu."

Penny made a rude noise. "Wimps like you three wouldn't even try."

Oh, I'd had the deadly puffer fish before. With Tomas in his penthouse in NYC. My heartbeat sped up remembering that wonderful week, the late night dinner, and the chef who had been called in for the special dish. There wasn't much of a taste to it at all.

I focused on my friends. Now wasn't the time to be thinking about Tomas. He didn't acknowledge my presence anymore. Why bother?

A round of sake came out first. With glee and a cackle, Penny placed each drink in front of us. "I got the good stuff. Junmai sake."

"Very nice." Sophie snatched hers quickly.

Griff rolled his eyes. How did he survive hanging out with those two while I was overseas?

"What do we say before we drink, Soph?" Penny asked.

"Say *kanpai*, which means dry the glass, then we sip—"

"I believe she said we drink like we want to get wasted," Penny added.

We did as instructed, shouting cheers before we slammed down the drinks. It was so fun. The drink burned a little going down, but overall the beverage was smooth.

Penny motioned for the waitress to fill us up again.

"Again?" Sophie muttered.

"Like you can't handle your liquor." Penny rubbed her hands while I scanned the restaurant. The place was pretty packed.

Once the waitress came back, Sophie ordered a spring roll and I hurriedly added a rainbow roll.

"What are you doing?" Penny said. "Stop being an old bitch and let's have some fun!"

Old bitch? She was a year older than me.

"I still want the roll, but I want the small one," I said to the waitress. I wasn't stupid.

We didn't have to wait long for the first plate to arrive. I tilted my head and leaned in for a closer look. It was fleshy, white, and resembled cauliflower.

"What the fuck?" I mumbled.

"Oh, *shirako no sashimi!*" Sophie looked pleased.

Griffin not so much.

Penny grinned like she couldn't wait for me to try it. "You have traveled so much, I had to research overtime with Sophie here to make sure you hadn't tried this before."

"No shit . . ." I picked up my chopsticks and took a deep breath. There was a small bowl of gluten-free soy sauce next to the food, ready for dipping. If I dared to eat. No matter what, I was trying it.

With practiced ease, Sophie tore off a portion using her chopsticks and dipped the piece in the soy sauce. Thick, white stuff oozed from the place where she tore off her piece.

"I'm gonna pass." Griffin picked up his drink and sipped.

"Your turn." Penny turned to me, her black eyes glittering with mischief.

I wasn't one to turn down a dare, so I took a small portion and put it in my mouth. It was strangely chewy like gelatin. Also the portion was a bit buttery, with a hint of a briny taste. "What part of the fish is this? This tastes like week-old tuna."

"It's the sperm sac of a cod fish," Penny declared with pride.

The food solidified in my mouth.

"A fish *spunk holder?*" I kept chewing and swallowed. There was no way I was letting Penny win this game.

I even got some more. *Bring it, baby.*

"So what's next?" I asked.

The next round, which came before I had a chance to have more *shirako,* was practically alive. Still moving squid squirmed on three sticks in two bowls. I tried not to stare too hard as a rather hardy squid attempted to make a daring escape from a bowl of gluten-free soy sauce.

Sophie picked up a stick with a squid wrapped around it first. She squeezed her eyes tight and ate. Disgust rolled across her face, even as she tried to chew as quickly as possible. "Ugh!"

Just as fast as she closed her mouth, she opened it again to try to spit it out. I shuddered from the sight.

"The ten . . . tacles. Ugh! They . . . keep getting stuck in my mouth." Finally, she spit out the rest into a napkin. "Even I have a limit," she managed. "That thing's not going down without a fight."

Everyone turned and looked at me.

Penny picked up the squid—drenched in soy sauce— and extended the stick in my direction. "Your turn."

I took what she offered. The writhing food lingered near my lips, and all I could think about was the horror on Sophie's face. I'd bet I had a squirmer on my hands.

Here goes nothing.

I sucked in the whole thing, making sure I downed some water to help.

It was one of the creepiest things I'd ever eaten in my life.

The others erupted into cheers around me.

"Now that's what I like to see!" Penny said with gusto. "Want a second one?"

"I'll pass. I need to eat some real food, too." I grabbed a bowl of rice and took a few bites. Maybe that would help me forget about the squid.

"How have you been feeling lately? Your new diet helping?" Sophie asked.

"Yeah, I've been meaning to ask you that," Penny added. "I was surprised when you told us you had celiac disease over the phone."

"What's celiac disease again?" Griffin asked.

"One of my clients has it," Sophie explained. "They can't absorb gluten—that's wheat, rye—that kind of thing. If my client eats gluten she doesn't feel well because gluten causes an autoimmune reaction in her body. Her diagnosis came after her physician noticed she was becoming too thin." The others at the table switched their focus from Sophie to me. "Which is why she looks like she lost weight," she added.

"I'm feeling better. I had a pretty bad iron deficiency when I left the UK and I was tired all the time." I took a sip of the sake. "I thought I was stressed out about my job and finding my parents, but it was my illness instead."

Penny rested her head on my shoulder briefly. "We got your back now. We are your family. We fight together. We protect each other."

I nodded as Griffin placed his hand on my other shoulder. Across from me Sophie smiled.

"I don't know about the fight together part—" Griffin began.

"Shut it," Penny snapped. "We're bonding here. I only ran away from a fight once."

Griffin's right eyebrow rose. "Those kids off 69th Street were no joke. They beat my ass, waited twenty minutes, and then beat me down again—"

Penny grimaced. "I know! You don't have to remind me."

"We're gonna be crotchety old folks getting sponge baths and I will still bring this up," he added.

Sophie winked and nodded. "Yeah, I would, too."

Penny laughed a bit and finished off her drink. "I'm going to the ladies room. We need a quieter place where we can talk and drink." She gave me her usual mischievous Penny grin. "You ready for round two at another bar?"

"Maybe the question should be whether you're ready?" I replied.

Penny headed to the bathroom while Griffin and Sophie tried to wrangle the squid back into the bowl. They had made some progress while I offered Kentucky Derby-style commentary.

Soon enough, Penny returned and motioned for the waitress. When she asked for the bill, the waitress grinned. "It's already been paid. A gentleman saw your birthday party and wanted to treat everyone."

"Wow." Sophie stood first to look around.

I did the same, not recognizing a single soul.

"Cheers to our benefactor 'cause I was about to drop half a paycheck on you." Penny downed Sophie's full cup. "The guy who paid better not be waiting outside my apartment . . ."

I glanced around the restaurant again, and for a brief moment, I considered the possibility of Tomas being here, but the idea was so ludicrous I tossed the thought aside. He didn't know I was here, nor did he care.

Chapter Fourteen

Carlie

Around two a.m., I'd stumbled into my minuscule apartment—only slightly drunk.

I wouldn't call myself drunk. More like slightly inebriated, just enough to make poor decisions. Like *not* setting my alarm clock.

As to be expected, I got to work two hours late. Not only did I wake up with my mouth open, but my skirt from last night was on backwards and my tangled hair was a hot mess. I scrambled to wash my face and brush my hair. I had time for little else.

I snuck into work, with horribly wrinkled clothes befitting a night of drunken disregard, and I hoped Mr. Butts wasn't lying in wait to question my tardiness. I hurried to cram my purse into my employee locker. My head pounded a bit and within my fog, perhaps I could believe I was holding a balloon in my hand. Someone had stuffed a balloon into my locker, along with a small bouquet of pink dahlias.

Another gift from my friends?

There was no way the concierge desk would leave these things in here though. I checked the bouquet and found a small card inside: "Happy birthday from Mr. Goodfellow."

My heart jumped into my throat.

So he had remembered.

I plucked everything out of the locker and took them back to my desk. All the while, I couldn't shake the questions in my head.

None of them would be answered unless I confronted Tomas, but that couldn't be done until my break time. I hurried to Dante's Second Floor and checked the concierge desks. I hadn't missed anything. Thank goodness.

The hours slowly passed though. Headache medication lifted the fog in my brain, but I couldn't shake the need to know what was up. The moment my break came, I marched straight to his office on the third floor, ready to find out why he didn't come see me yesterday, but he wasn't there.

His secretary Wendy greeted me. "Mr. Goodfellow isn't available. You're Carlie, right?" Her smile was sweet for a woman I'd called very beautiful. "I hope you liked the gifts Mr. Goodfellow got for you."

"He went out and bought them?"

Wendy chuckled a bit. "Not really, but he told me what you liked. Also, that you loved dahlias and how you always wanted to get balloons on your birthday as a kid, but no one ever got them for you."

"Yeah." I wasn't sure what to say about that. All these years and he'd never sent me flowers or balloons on my birthday. An ocean had separated us, but this time he'd reached out to me, even after I'd pushed him away.

"He should be back around two p.m., if you'd like to come back?"

"I won't be able to get away again to see him." I took a step back to retreat.

"Why not right now then?" a deep voice said.

I turned around to see Tomas standing behind me.

Tomas

I approached Sophie. "If I hadn't escaped from my lunch meeting so early, I might've never had a chance to corner you."

The smell of her sweet perfume filled my nostrils and I wanted to draw her close to me.

"I have to get back to work," she murmured.

I shrugged. "But you just got here."

"I changed my mind. And anyway, Mr. Butts might need me."

"He'll be fine. I could write you a note, if you like."

She snorted and her nose lifted in that cute way I liked. "Are you a principal now?"

"Would you like for me to be?"

Her lips parted and she feigned disinterest and failed.

"Come into my office, Ms. Jason."

She followed me into my suite and closed the double doors after us.

"I didn't really want anything…I just wanted to thank you for the flowers and the balloons. That was very sweet."

I settled onto my white leather couch and beckoned for her to sit next to me. Instead of adding space between us, she sat with her left knee mere inches from mine.

"I still remember the day when I took you to that

birthday party." She didn't say anything while I spoke. "You didn't care about Andrea's lavish gifts—but the flowers caught your attention the most."

"It was a whole new world for me." She snorted. "Andrea had the nerve to think I was someone's assistant and not your date. How is she? Is she still living off her trust fund in Europe?"

"Pretty much, but that was her fate though." I turned to look at her. She was so beautiful I could look at her all day. "Can you imagine all the freedoms you have compared to Andrea though? All the money in the world won't buy you people who truly care about you. The only time she sees her family is when they feel like it. She has *acquaintances*. They spend time with her because of her pedigree and not her character."

We sat for a bit. "Have you eaten lunch yet?" I asked.

"I'm not hungry. I sort of ate on the run this morning."

"What did you have?" Yep, I was digging, but I knew she wouldn't reveal anything unless I cornered her. Yesterday at the sushi restaurant, I sat with my back to her small party and I overheard a *very* interesting conversation. I wanted to know more, but Carlie would clam up if I pushed too hard. Her health was important to me, so I decided to wait for her to make the first move.

"The standard fare for employees who run late: two yogurt parfaits, a Starbucks double shot energy drink, and I topped all that off with a rather large bag of mixed nuts." She didn't look at me while she replied.

"No bagel buried in cream cheese?"

She shook her head and glanced at me. "Those tend to weigh me down." Her eyes reflected the truth this time.

Her thick blonde hair followed the curve of her cheek. I didn't stop myself from drawing my finger along her jaw to tuck her hair behind her ear.

"Unlike two parfaits, a drink, and a bag of mixed nuts," I added.

Her voice trailed off. "Unlike two parfaits, a drink . . ."

She licked her lips and faced me. "I'd like to see you again."

"No text message this time?"

"We didn't exactly plan our last encounter."

So us having sex was an *encounter* now. At least, she wanted to spend time with me.

"No, we didn't, but that made the experience much more pleasurable."

I watched the way her chest rose and fell faster and the way her hands formed fists. When my fingertips brushed against the swell of her breast, she leaned toward my hand.

"Why meet tonight?" I breathed. "Why not right now?"

Chapter Fifteen

Carlie

I ached for him to hold me. All morning I couldn't stop thinking about him, from the minute I got up to the moment I walked through the door to the hotel. I wanted to do anything he wanted. As long as we were together.

"Right now?" I asked.

"Come here, Carlie." His request was a plea and not a command. I didn't hesitate to take off my heels and stand before him.

"Take off that skirt."

I unzipped my skirt and let it fall to the floor. The look in his eyes, as if he wanted to devour me, climbed up the back of my thighs and caressed along the middle of my back. He didn't give me long to stand there in only my shirt and panties. He drew me into his lap and forced my legs apart to straddle him. How wonderfully we fit together, his hands on my ass, my chest against his.

He pulled me closer until my forehead rested against

his mouth. A warm feeling filled my chest, and the comfort I needed for so long almost overwhelmed me.

I sucked in a breath from the divine pleasure of his lips brushing across my skin. My fingers drifted down his chest until my right hand rested over his pebbled nipple. One hard rub was a dare, but a continuous pressure was a promise. I wouldn't leave this time. I'd stay until the very end.

His lips lingered close to the bridge of my nose. We shared breaths now. A heavenly sigh snuck out of my mouth as he pushed my core against his cock. I wanted him. I wanted all of him over and over again.

I rocked against him and he gripped my ass harder until the pain was hard to take, but I didn't give in. I knew what was coming and I was ready to accept him. He was moving lower. Even lower until he brushed against my upper lip. He was so close I caught the mintiness of his warm breath. So teasingly close. I was so tempted to open my mouth and kiss back. Yet even when he ran his tongue along my upper lip, I didn't respond.

The moan I fought against reached painful levels. I'd give him everything except that.

Gently, he pulled me up to stand. Instead of yanking my underwear down, he slowly slipped my panties off, only to kiss the skin my panties touched. I stepped out of them. With deft practice, he unbuttoned my blouse and slid it off me. The hard look on his face told me I would enjoy what was about to happen.

Touch me, I wanted to beg. He was going too slow. *Taste me,* I wanted to scream.

The moment my bra came off, he latched onto one breast. Just watching him lick along my golden nipple ring sent a violent shudder down my back to my inner thighs.

His thumb penetrated me and I had to hold on to his shoulders to continue standing.

"Damn," I breathed.

"I might just give you what you want today."

"Really?"

He added a finger inside me. "If that's what I want."

I wanted to give him anything he wanted. Giving him pleasure gave me pleasure.

As quickly as my desire heightened, his tempo increased until he withdrew. Quickly, I fell to my knees and opened his pants. His length sprang forth and my eager mouth sucked in the tip.

I loved watching his reactions while I licked his cock. Every twitch made me want to take all of him deeper into my mouth. I ran my fingers along his length. Every single inch was magnificent. I took him deeper. Even as I gripped his muscular thighs, I trembled against him.

For a moment I pulled back, but he took a fistful of my hair and made me hold still. *That's it.* There was the Tomas I remembered. He pushed in and out of my mouth. Taking his pleasure as the tension in my scalp reached a blissful level.

Yes, I wanted all of it. All the pain and pleasure.

I handed myself over to him. He pumped faster to the point where I could barely breathe. My limbs grew weak, but I continued to suck, I continued to watch him watch me. His beautiful brown eyes taking me in. Watching me pleasure him. His body stiffened, but he didn't climax.

He pulled me back onto his lap on the couch. I slid down onto his length, my body shuddering from being filled up. It was always like this between us. A feverish heat that left my blood heated, my heart pounding, and a sheen of sweat along my back.

I rode him, rising and falling with our quickening

breaths. Pressure built in my stomach. Damn, he filled me with each downward stroke until I was panting.

I rested against the crook of his neck, my favorite place to ride out the oncoming climax, but he wouldn't allow it.

He pushed me backward.

I was back in the position I didn't want to be in. Chest to chest. His mouth close to mine. The heat between us rose higher and higher, the sounds of our bodies meeting filling the large space. I grabbed his shoulders, unable to hold back my rising cries.

He nibbled against my chin again. My gaze flicked to his and the look he gave me sent me crashing under the waves.

~

Tomas

Her lips were a witches' brew I wanted to resist today, but I couldn't fight against the need to kiss her. Watching her suck my cock had been torture. Even harder was when she'd licked my nipples and suckled along my skin.

Those delicious lips beckoned me to sample them. To devour them.

If I told her to kiss me, she would without a doubt.

But I didn't want that. I wanted all of her.

Her body gripped my cock to the point of agony. She closed her eyes briefly, and I took in her features. The way her thick hair beckoned me to run my fingers through it. The glossy tingle to her lips when she licked them. I wanted to take that lower lip into my mouth and suck on it.

I settled for her jaw instead.

Then her neckline.

I sampled her skin in the places she wanted me to

touch. All the while, I lingered near the place I really wanted to be. The corner of her mouth. The indentation below her lower lip. I sucked, nipped, and tickled.

The tension building along my thighs toward my cock grew painful. Above me, Carlie's beautiful face stretched into a grimace and she climaxed, her body tensing and her eyes glowing from finding bliss.

"That's it, *Coraçao*."

I wasn't far behind her. I drew her close to me again. Our bodies worked as one. A sensual dance where the beginning and ending of our bodies met. This would have to do. This wonderful feeling I had knowing I'd be able to hold her close like this. She'd run away from me again, but for now, as I shuddered and reached my climax, she belonged to me, body and soul.

Chapter Sixteen

Carlie

Leaving my employer's office after having sex with him wasn't the experience I'd expected on the day after my birthday, but I had to admit I had a bit of a skip to my step on the way to the elevator.

For the rest of the day I was in a haze. Focusing on work was near to impossible and he kept texting me.

Tomas: *You left your jacket in my office.*

Me: *I'll get it later, I'm working.*

Another one came as I was checking the library. *You can come and get it now if you like.*

Me: *I'm sure I could get right back on your lap, too.*

Tomas: *Multiple times I guarantee.*

I laughed like a fool in front of Mr. Ericson in the library.

He had a rather nice tan today.

By the time I was ready to finish up for the day, he sent me another text. *I can see you won't be fetching your jacket, so I had it dry-cleaned. You'll find it in your locker tomorrow morning.*

I texted back thanks and was grateful he didn't ask for more of my time. Parting was always the hardest thing between us.

My lips tingled as I recalled the last time we'd kissed. Damn, I'd dodged a bullet. Good thing I hadn't kissed him. When we'd parted last time, I remembered the pain from crying so hard. The way his lips tasted and how I didn't want to remember how good it felt to share something so intimate with someone.

My day brightened a bit more when I saw Carver motion me over to chat with him. He was his relaxed self in a dark purple T-shirt and blue jeans. The shoelaces for his Timberland boots lay pooled around his feet.

He smiled at me and the burdens I carried lifted a bit. "Hey, Jason!"

"What's up?"

He slowly grinned. "I know you didn't want my help . . ."

"No, I didn't." I immediately knew where this was going, but it was hard for me to be mad about it.

"I had my boys do some looking and I've got some good news for you. According to my guy, he's narrowed down the number of Patricia Halls to three. He's followed two of them and figured out that one of them wasn't your mother."

"How was that?"

"You don't look Dominican to me."

"So? There are white people there."

"Good point—but this particular woman looked *nothing* like you."

I snorted.

He was quiet for a bit. When I moved to leave, he spoke up. "I do have more news for you . . . I wasn't sure how to bring it up."

My heart sank. "What's wrong?"

"I found Frank Hall, your father."

Dread sucked me in, and I knew what he was about to say before he spoke. "He's dead, isn't he?"

He nodded. "I'm sorry, Carlie. We found a death certificate."

I hurried to change the subject. Mourning the loss of my dad would happen tonight when I could be alone. "So what about the last two? Can I get an address? Maybe check it out on my own?"

His eyebrow rose. "Are you sure? You just found out—"

"Why not?"

He slowly nodded, understanding. "Got any time off coming soon?"

"What do you mean?"

"We could go check it out."

"Only with dinner and a movie, too?"

"Not really, I'm not the movie type."

I chuckled. "You're more live action."

He tilted his head when a woman across the room smiled at him from her group of friends. "You could say that."

"Look, I've got Tuesday off. I owe a friend of mine a shopping trip so how about we go after that?" I picked up his old drink since I had a fresh one to place. I'd be back in an hour with another refill.

"Sounds good."

I pushed his fresh cup of green goo his way. "Drink up, Carver. I can't have you passing out on me since you snuck some pie this morning."

"Your kitchen is full of traitors."

I took a step back and tried to fight the rising discomfort in my stomach. Carver's news was finally sinking in. "Thanks again for everything."

"Not a problem. Stan's happy he doesn't have to chase after deadbeats for a while." He shrugged.

I turned away to take the drink back to the kitchen. When I glanced over my shoulder briefly, I caught Carver looking away.

HOURS later I'd bought a large bouquet of white lilies and a bottle of red wine. Doing a private memorial for a man I didn't know proved difficult that night. I would've liked to have thought I had more in me than the flowers and wine, but that's what I had. Damn, I wished I could cook something nicer than microwaved rice and baked fish.

With everything arranged nicely on my tiny kitchenette table, I turned on my TV and switched the channel to ESPN. I mean hey, why not? If my dad were like me, he'd appreciate a good time watching hockey instead of a dried-up drama on the next channel.

I touched the dahlias from Tomas fondly and managed a half smile. The two flowers looked beautiful next to each other. The contrasting colors of pink and white brightened the edges of my sadness creeping in.

"Here's looking at you, Dad . . ." I raised my glass of port to the flowers and then took a drink. On the second sip, my glass didn't make it to my mouth as a singular thought slammed into my gut: *I didn't even get a chance to say hello.*

The pain hurt worst than one of my stomachaches.

I didn't even have a picture of him to recall his face. I didn't even have any tears to give him, either.

A tiny bite of food reached my mouth and I couldn't eat anymore. My throat grew too dry and I wiped away a single tear. One meal, maybe even two would've been nice.

For a little while, I imagined him sitting across from me. He might've had red hair like mine and his forehead wrinkled as he laughed. His tattoos on his forearms were hard to make out, but like anyone with ink, his told a story I loved hearing about again and again. He'd eaten my slightly dry fish and made jokes about my kind of burnt rice—but he'd eat it all cause he was cool like that.

The TV grew loud as a fistfight between two players broke out and I smiled wistfully.

"We should do this more often, Dad," I whispered.

TWO DAYS LATER, as I promised Penny and Lana, we went out to lunch and browsed a few shops beforehand. Promise wasn't the right word. Perhaps coerced would be better. They let me choose our lunch—and I couldn't wait to try an Italian restaurant off Boylston Street near the Boston Public Garden. With near perfect skies and the expansive view of the gardens across the street, I basked in the glow of my friends' company.

"Oh, c'mon," Penny spouted as she devoured the final bites of her chicken parmesan. "The least you can do is spend some time with me. I had to reschedule a few key clients today."

Lana grinned. She dug into her coq du vin with gusto. The pretty redhead was Sophie and Penny's roommate and a first-year medical student who tagged along for a free meal.

I glanced down at my plate. The gluten-free chicken noodle soup here was divine! I hid a smile from the others. Lately, I'd been feeling so much better. To combat my malnourishment issues, I took my supplements everyday from my doc in the UK and I monitored my diet.

Changing my eating habits took a bit of time, but now that I'd taken a new course in life I had far more energy than before.

I felt like conquering the world.

Love, not so much.

While they were eating, I got Penny caught up on my search for my parents.

"I'm so sorry about your dad," Penny said as she scraped the bottom of her plate. "At least you're one step closer to finding your mom."

After taking a sip of her water, she added, "How do you like working at Goodfellow Tower?"

"It's fine. Just another hotel," I replied.

"You sound bored." The waiter took Penny's plate, but that didn't stop her from chatting away. "Why not look for a different job?"

"I just want to find my mother and get back to the UK. I'm meeting this guy in a bit to go check out someone."

"Sounds exciting," Lana added. "Maybe this lady will be your mom."

I couldn't help smiling from the warm feeling I kept having at the thought.

"Maybe she might be—but don't let your heart get broken. Just because you can find her doesn't mean she wants to be found—" Penny began.

"Don't do this shit," I said, trying to sound nice. "This is important to me, Penny." Over the years, I'd gotten a less than an enthusiastic response from Penny and Sophie. Neither of them expressed an interest about their origins.

"Those people abandoned you," Penny used to quip. *"The way I see it, my bios did me a favor when they left me wandering the streets."* Sophie's mom had left her at the hospital, but my situation was different. I had been left in foster care around

eight months. Which meant for several months, my mother had held me, fed me when I'd cried, and loved me.

That's what I wanted to believe.

Fifteen minutes later, we wrapped up lunch, but Penny's words weighed heavily on me. Lana said her good-byes and ran to catch a bus while Penny lingered with her chatty self. As usual.

I caught Carver coming around the corner. He strode up to us wearing a white T-shirt and jeans. His usual ensemble for Dante's Second Floor.

I turned to Penny and whispered, "Okay, so I don't want to keep you. I'm sure there's somebody with a boner waiting for your call—"

"Hey, Carlie." He towered over all of us—even tall, modelesque Penny.

She glanced from me to Carver. The sly grin on her face widened. "Is this the friend you're meeting?"

"Yeah." I introduced Penny to Carver Murphy.

She reached out, and they shook hands. "Nice, big hands," she remarked.

Oh, hell the fuck no. She used the *voice.* This guy was a client at my hotel and not one of her phone sex customers.

I faked checking my cellphone. "Looks like we should get going."

"My car is around the corner," Carver said. He looked Penny up and down with interest and I tried to hold back a laugh. With Carver in front of me, I couldn't fill Penny in on what kind of man he was, but they were grown-ass adults, they'd figure it out.

"Mind if I tag along?" Penny asked. "For moral support, of course."

"Do you mind?" I asked him. Penny was one of my besties. As long as she behaved.

"Not a problem." He led us back to his black Lincoln Navigator and he got into the driver's seat.

Boylston Street was packed with cars. I was surprised he'd found a parking space.

As I slid into the front passenger seat, I saw the look of pure joy on Penny's face and shook my head with a smile. Who was I to deny her some man candy?

"What's that smell?" I asked. The whole interior, from the polished leather seats to the pimped out dashboard, smelled minty with a hint of something saccharine.

"That's spiced candy. The kind you get during Christmas." He headed north until we hit Storrow Drive.

As we drove west down the six-lane street, I asked about the smell. "Why not new car smell?" I asked with a laugh.

"You're asking the man with a sugar addiction why his car smells like this?"

Good point.

We drove for a bit and I couldn't stop my hands from shaking so I placed them in my lap. "So where are we going?"

"You'll see." His smile was reassuring. "Are you sure you want to come along?"

"I've been waiting so long to do this." Even Penny's jokes wouldn't pry me from this car.

For the rest of the way, we drove in silence to the southwest—until Penny sent me a text message: *hey c, has tall, dark, and tasty got a girlfriend?*

Me: *I dunno. I don't ask that kind of thing.*

Penny: *oh lawd, he is fine. I just want to rub his bald head against my tits.*

Me: *you are so wrong for that . . .*

Penny: *don't be mad 'cause my rack is bigger than yours.*

Me: *whatever, just be nice to him.*

From the corner of my eye, I caught Penny's fingers creeping up the side of the seat. She'd almost reached his arm when Carver spoke up.

"How long have you two known each other?" he asked me.

"Since we were kids. We grew up together," I replied.

"So where did you meet Carlie?" Penny asked. She knew damn well where I'd met him and pried like a pro.

"I travel a lot, but for the past couple of weeks I've been staying at the hotel where your friend works," he said.

"Oh, really." She leaned forward in the seat, placing her hands on his shoulders. Penny was practically straining against the seat belt. "Even though I work from home, I adore traveling. Where do you hail from?"

"Chicago born and bred. And you?"

"New York City. I miss it sometimes and go back a few times a year."

The two continued to gab, but when Carver turned off onto Elm Street in the Sumner Hill neighborhood of Jamaica Plain, my breath quickened and sweat lined my palms. Their conversation faded away and I took in every thing. Was this my mom and dad's neighborhood? Had they lived here for years before my dad passed away? This historic district was one of the nicer ones. Not as well-to-do as Back Bay, but if my mom lived here that meant she'd done well for herself.

From one tree-lined street to another, turn after turn, anticipation built in my stomach.

Finally, we reached a street with a beautiful cobblestone wall. All the houses along this street, many of them offset from the road, were breathtaking, ornate Italianate-style homes. I've always been a sucker for classical architecture. Our final destination was a beautiful mustard yellow house, with dark brown trim, sheltered among oak trees. The lot wasn't too big, but the small circular driveway boasted the owner's wealth.

Carver got out of the car first and I motioned that I wanted to follow.

"Stay here," he said. "Let me check things out first."

"Please," I grabbed his arm. The thick muscle under my palm flexed. "I won't say anything. Even if she doesn't want to meet me, I'd like to see her."

He didn't move and continued to look at the house as if he considered what I'd asked him. I spoke again before he could change his mind. "I promise to behave."

In the backseat, I caught Penny shaking her head. For once, she was silent.

Carver took the lead and I followed him up the cobblestone path. Just seeing the tri-level house up close left me in awe. This place had to be in the millions of dollars. Was my mother loaded?

He walked up to the double red doors and knocked. I swallowed down my apprehension and waited to see who would answer the door. Would a haughty butler answer?

A short Indian woman answered and my disappointment was immediate. "Can I help you?" she asked.

"I'm sorry to disturb you, but we're looking for Patricia Hall. I work for a private investigation firm."

The woman's face scrunched up with concern. "I'm sorry but if you have any legal matters for me, you should contact my husband." She took a step back and the door closed a bit.

She wasn't my birth mother.

Carver took a step back and I trailed after him. Now that I thought about it, a stranger walking up to my house and asking for me would creep me out, too. "No problem. We meant no harm. Thank you, Mrs. Hall, for your time."

My feet shuffled on the pavement during our trip back

to the car. Instead of getting into the seat, I wanted to keep going. A headache formed at the back of my skull and the feeling of disappointment settled into my chest.

"We've still got two more people to check out," Carver said softly.

I forced a smile on my face. "That means she might be out there."

He tapped my shoulder. "That's what I like to hear, Jason."

I was headed home empty-handed, but at least the buoyancy of my spirits remained high.

Chapter Seventeen

Carlie

J ust two more mystery women separated me from learning about my mom and I refused to let Carver's people make the introductions without me—which meant I needed another day off soon.

Toss in a conference on domesticated dog reproduction and you've got one busy chick.

As usual, my alarm clocks didn't go off as expected. The siren noise, which got me a complaint from my neighbors, didn't do its job to drop kick me out of slumber.

I stumbled out of bed and hurried to get a dose of coffee. Not long after I'd arrived, I loaded up on healthy food from an organic store nearby. As of today, a lot of that food was gone. I needed a plan instead of winging it though. My bank account had taken a hit, but my improved health was worth it. In the last few weeks, my life had changed in so many ways. I scratched the side of my face and prepared my coffee. The aroma filled the room and I perked up a bit. I was definitely a caffeine junkie.

After my first sip, I couldn't help but think about the mornings before today when I used to eat muffins. Or even pancakes with Tomas.

I shoved those thoughts away and hurried to get dressed. I wouldn't be able to afford to stay here if I didn't make money. I threw on my heels and dabbed a bit of perfume on my wrists. With little time to spare, I scampered out the door.

"Consult a dietitian while you're in the US, Ms. Jason," my physician had reminded me.

I was taking better care of myself, but a few things, like Tomas, I tried to push aside.

By the time I reached the hotel, the place was packed with conference attendees standing in line. All the clerks were present, but just seeing how busy things were told me I wouldn't see my mother any time soon.

Two hours later, I was in the middle of the madness at the hotel and I was a bit tired. The line never seemed to end and conference attendees were out-of-towners. Their needs ranged from last minute tickets to the Boston Opera House to exclusive arrangements at the premier golf courses. Could I make arrangements for a family of six to visit the aquarium? Maybe I could help with a seafood dinner for a party of sixteen? Half of the time, the hardest part about working during a conference was remembering the needs of each client and reacting appropriately when you saw them again.

Not once did I see Tomas.

He was the hotel owner though, what reason did he have to be on the front lines with the soldiers.

As hard as I tried to tell myself I didn't care, I couldn't shake the anticipation as I walked around each corner.

Once the line at the check-in desk was under control, I had to make sure another group of buyers for the Tower would arrive to the conference room for another meeting. That meant a few phone calls to their assistants, or in this case, one of the buyers who didn't have one. "*Bien sûr,* Monsieur Denis. I'll take you to the meeting personally if you'd like."

Mr. Denis thanked me for my help and ended the call. I had a few minutes to take a breather before I had to fetch him.

"Who are the bigwigs this time?" Yolanda asked me between phone calls. She was on her break and eating a snack.

"More businessmen. This time from Canada." I checked my cellphone messages for the ninth time. I had two more new ones.

"Are you all right?" Yolanda asked me with a grin. "I haven't seen you around lately."

"Yeah, what's wrong?"

"You seem nervous for some reason." Her grin was sly.

"Oh, stop it. I just have a lot on my mind today."

"Yeah, a lot on your mind."

"I've seen you work a lot and you seem so cool and relaxed. It's rather scary if I think about it." She leaned in, her eyes dancing with mischief. "Seeing you lose your cool is kinda refreshing."

Had I been that obvious? I straightened my back. "Let's just get this done so we can have some lunch. I'm about to tackle one of those cardboard sandwiches the staff abandoned in the break room."

After I fetched Mr. Denis from his suite on the thirty-ninth floor, we arrived to the conference room where many of the other guests had already assembled.

"Is there anything else I can do for you?" I asked him in French, hoping I hadn't messed up any words.

"*No thank you.*" He left my side to greet the other buyers

from his team. I looked over the room. Most of the executives from Gold Bridge Construction had the same look. The stiff collars and confident expressions. I walked through the room and checked the beverage and lunch tables to make sure everything was in place. All I had to do was sweep the room and make sure everyone had what they needed and then I could go.

Then I noticed him standing across the room. He was beautiful, practically a lion among his pride. He stood with two buyers discussing the many features of the hotel. None of them included Dante's Second Floor, but what he said reflected his pride. Just listening to him made me heady. If he moved me so much, how come I felt this way? Why was I ready to bolt and run away? Just thinking about our time together in his office still made my stomach quiver.

The group he was with headed toward the beverage table. He separated briefly from them to speak to the lady manning the table. He walked right past me without saying a word. At other times, he at least acknowledged me, but this time, nothing.

A lump formed in my throat and I tried to swallow it down.

Wasn't this what you wanted, Carlie? Our intimate moments would stay locked away. Also, I wasn't willing to give into him and this was exactly what I needed—a boundary formed between us he didn't cross.

I scanned the room and smoothed down my skirt. The body language of everyone in the room comforted me. No one needed me.

Not even him.

Chapter Eighteen

Carlie

Thankfully, after the conference ended I managed to take a day off. I really wanted to venture out again with Carver to check out the lead on another Patricia Hall.

This time he picked me up at my place around ten in the morning. Any earlier and I would've been comatose.

The inside of his SUV smelled like coffee and candy.

"Hey, Jason," he said. "I got you some black coffee."

The aroma was wonderful. "I didn't know what you liked," he added, "so I grabbed a bunch of creamers and sugars."

"You got enough sugar here to bake a cake." I chuckled and added some cream and sugar to my coffee.

"I needed some, too."

Uh-huh.

I feigned glancing at my watch. "So how long do I have until you go into diabetic shock?"

"I'm doing pretty good today."

My smile faltered. He hadn't been around Dante's Second Floor in the last few days. "Has something come up or . . ."

"I was in the hospital for a bit. Not too long." He flashed me a beautiful smile and I had to grin in return.

"You okay?" I asked.

"Drinking that green stuff every day only goes so far."

"True that."

"I've been working long shifts and that shit catches up with you eventually. My doctor says I will be out of commission for a while since I need more testing."

"And you're out with me today? What are you thinking?"

"I'm not an invalid. I just need to take better care of myself."

"Hence long trips to Dante's Second Floor for people watching."

"Exactly."

I groaned. "Where are we going?"

"Cleveland Heights. My lookout told me she showed up a few days ago. She hadn't been home since then. They said she looked—a bit ill."

"Ill?"

"Yeah, like she'd been sick."

"That's not good."

Just like last time, my heart was deep in my throat, even to the point when we pulled up to the brown brick two-story home. Was this the place where my mom lived? I tried not to get my hopes up. I was in a better place compared to last time.

Carver went first and walked up to the door. He knocked a few times, but no one showed up. Finally, after a few minutes, a woman opened the door. She looked nothing like me though. Her hair was dark brown and her skin tone was a few shades darker.

She smiled at Carver. "Can I help you? Sorry it took me so long."

"I'm so sorry to bother you, ma'am." He introduced himself as a private investigator. "We're looking for Patricia Hall."

"That's me." Concern lined her features.

"My client is looking for a relative and, well, we're so sorry to disturb you today." He took a step back.

"Wait a minute," the woman said. She peeked at me as I stood on the sidewalk. My heartbeat grew painful. "You're looking for Patty, right? About the height of that girl there, same face?"

I hurried to the door. "Yes, I am. That's my mom."

The woman laughed a bit and she leaned on the door. "I can't stand up too long, but you can come in for a bit if you like."

"We can wait here. We don't want to intrude," Carver said.

"Don't worry. Ace trusts you." I peered behind Patricia and saw a huge German Shepherd. The dog wagged his tail.

We walked into the small house and Carver closed the door behind him. The place was sparsely furnished and newspapers were scattered across one of the blue couches.

"The home care lady isn't coming until tomorrow so you'll have to pardon my mess," the lady said.

"No problem." I picked up the newspapers and placed them into a pile. My hands were shaking the whole time.

"So you know Patricia Hill who looks like my client Ms. Jason?" Carver began.

"Yeah, I get chemotherapy every two weeks at the medical center north of here. A few months ago, I happened to notice that the lady sitting next to me had the same name." Patricia smiled. "We always joked to the nurses that they better not mess up our meds."

Oh no.

"A cancer center." My voice sounded hollow.

Patricia nodded. "I shouldn't be spreading Patty's business to strangers, but yes, she has cancer. She looks just like you, though. It's the eyes and the face. I knew the moment I saw you that you're related to her."

"My mom gave me up and left me in a foster home."

"And now you're looking for her," Patricia finished.

I nodded, unsure what I could say to get Patricia to give me more information. I opened my mouth again, but Carver spoke first.

"If you wouldn't mind telling us where you're treated, we can look on our own. We don't want to put you in an uncomfortable position."

"I don't mind. Patty's always came by herself. You see, my son or my daughter-in-law takes me to chemo, but Patty was always alone. That bothered me to no end. It seemed like she was holding something dark inside and no matter how much I prayed for her, she seemed withdrawn."

"Cancer can do that to people. My best friend died from leukemia when I was a kid," Carver said.

"I'm sorry for your loss." Patricia sighed. "Every two weeks I saw her at the Blessed Faith Medical Center."

"So we might find her there?" I asked, eager to see her and find out if she'd be well or not. Please let her be better.

"Not anymore, honey. Patty told me two weeks ago she was going in for bowel surgery. She's still likely in the hospital. As to her current condition, I don't know."

Chapter Nineteen

Carlie

Once in a while, when I had a brief moment to myself, I dreamed that I was standing in a park next to my mother and we were feeding bread to the ducks. The wind off the bay brought crisp air, but my mother shielded me from the worst of it. Winter was coming, but I had nothing to fear.

Today, instead of that fantasy, I was sitting at my desk, feeling like I was a leaf about to be separated from the tree I clung to.

Yesterday, Carver had said, "If you give me about twenty-four hours, I can use my resources to find her."

I didn't remember nodding. It didn't matter though. I would've gone room to room if necessary. Especially now that I was so close to finding her.

As promised, while I was at work, my phone dinged with a new text: *Crestwood Memorial, room 4608. Take things slow. Tell anyone who asks that you're her daughter from out of town & you found out she had surgery. Good luck, Jason.*

Carver did it!

I nearly dropped the phone. I was that overwhelmed.

Somehow, I stumbled to the elevator and hurried up to Tomas's office. He was inside and didn't say anything when I drew his arms around me.

"Are you all right?" he asked.

"I am now," I murmured.

When I pulled away, he didn't say anything, only holding on to my hand until I let go of him. I wanted to tell him everything, but now wasn't the time.

"Recharged," I whispered. "Thank you."

I couldn't keep doing this to him. I couldn't do this to myself, either.

I tried to escape, but he held on to me.

"You've been keeping things from me. What's wrong?" he finally asked.

I tried to pull back, but he wouldn't budge. I bit my lower lip and my chin quivered. *Not now, Carlie.*

I refused to turn around and have him see me like this, but instead of letting me walk away, his grip grew stronger. Tomas pulled me into his arms, even when I stiffened.

"What's wrong, Carlie?" he asked again. Much more softly this time.

My teeth gnashed together and all my burdens slowly ebbed away. The walls I surrounded myself with crashed down into crumble. I'd told him I didn't need him anymore and here I was, clinging to him as if I was a ship seeking a safe harbor.

Owing you anything is a burden I'm not too good at carrying.

Why had I said that to him?

"I found her." My voice wasn't mine. I'd been hollowed out too many times.

"Your mom?"

"Yeah." That was all I could manage to say. As much

as I didn't want to rest my head on his chest, I did. This was the place I wanted to be right now. I could give in this one time.

I closed my eyes.

"Did she reject you?" His voice hardened.

I shook my head. "It's not like that. She's . . . in the hospital. She just had surgery for bowel cancer."

He cursed against the top of my head. "She gonna be okay?"

"I don't know. I haven't even gone yet."

He pulled back to cup my face with his large hands. "What are you doing here?"

"I had to work—I just found out."

He reached into his pocket and pulled out his handkerchief. He wiped my tears off my cheeks. After he did that, I wanted to hold him even longer. "Thank you," I managed.

"How about you take a breather, and then we'll go see her."

It wasn't a question. He had declared his intention to go with me.

"I can't have you do that. You have buyers coming today."

"I *did* have buyers coming today."

THE LAST TIME I'd been in a hospital, I was there for the test results of my celiac disease. Just like in the UK, hospitals were dry, sterile places you never wanted to visit.

Crestwood Memorial felt that way, but this time I wasn't alone. Tomas walked beside me. The feeling was strange, but I welcomed it. Our hands brushed a few times, but when I tried to move mine away he took it and squeezed it.

"I-I'm fine," I stammered.

"I know."

We didn't say much on the way up to room 4608. Tomas wasn't much for small talk and this time I appreciated it. My hands were sweaty and the sour feeling in my stomach heightened with each floor we passed. The moment was coming and I was scared shitless.

All this time I'd expected to see a woman standing in the flesh behind a closed door. She was supposed to invite me into her home and we'd catch up over tea. But, instead, I was walking down a quiet hallway with open doors and nurses sitting quietly at stations.

Take it slow, Carver had said.

Instead of hurrying, I crept up to the doorway and took a deep breath. There would be no mishaps this time. Someone was lying in the bed. I walked inside, my chest swelling with pain from my held breath.

"Hello?" I whispered.

There was no reply. I walked further inside and realized the patient was sleeping. The woman who was my mother lay still in the bed, her face ashen among her wrinkles and lines. A feeding tube circled her ear and ran into her nose. I could see myself, even in her withered appearance. Cancer had siphoned away the life from her limbs. The only sound in the room was her quiet breathing and the steady beeps of the machinery monitoring her well-being.

Somehow, I willed my feet to take a step closer. The pressure of Tomas's hand on my back faded away. Three more feet. Then two.

By the time I placed my hands on the railing, my legs were numb.

Her hands were so small, but her fingers were long— just like mine.

I waited, glancing at the doorway to make sure no one was coming and pondering how could I steal this moment.

Tomas stood on the far wall, his face encouraging.

I reached for her hand, expecting the skin to be cold, but her hand was quite warm.

"Hello," I somehow whispered.

I wasn't sure how long I stood there, but I started when someone spoke to me. "Can I help you?"

The nurse looked at me with concern.

My mouth flapped a bit before I spoke. "I'm her daughter."

The concern on the nurse's face flared before she peered at me closer. "She's not accepting visitors right now post-surgery."

"I-I'm sorry." I probably sounded like a babbling fool.

Tomas stepped forward. "Ms. Jason just heard about her mother's procedure, so she came here to check on her well-being."

"I see. So far Patty hasn't had any visitors."

"My mom and I are estranged." That was putting it lightly.

Tomas placed his hand on my shoulder. "We came to check on her. Is she receiving all the care she needs?"

"I can't share too much with you until I get permission from Patty, but she is resting comfortably."

I nodded, a bit reassured.

"Thanks." Tomas asked a few questions. All of them simple and nonintrusive. With that stolen minute I continued to take in her face. Every single feature I locked away in my mind. I'd found her. I'd finally found her.

I wiped away my tear and turned away.

"How soon can she come back to check on her mother?" Tomas asked.

"In a day or two, she should be up. After the procedure, we want to make sure she recovers comfortably."

He nodded.

Reluctantly, I left the room with Tomas, but I'd be back soon enough.

Chapter Twenty

Tomas

Watching Carlie look at her mother for the first time was an experience I'd never forget. Seeing her tremble with fear made me want to protect her and make that moment perfect.

I stood in front of the window at my penthouse, looking over the Boston skyline. So far all the lights had yet to give me any answers.

This was all supposed to be so simple. That was my thought when I hired someone to retrieve the address for Frank and Patricia Hall, but apparently the place had been abandoned. So far she'd done a fine job of searching on her own. She refused to tell me how she'd learned her father was dead and how she'd found her mom, though.

It didn't matter, though. Her mother had cancer and surgery to remove a part of her bowels. Helping Mrs. Hall was all that mattered.

Using my resources—even if Carlie didn't want my help—I contacted a colleague of mine at the hospital to give me some additional details. I hesitated twice before I called her up. She'd want to know—even if she didn't want my help. The phone was merely a communication tool for booty calls.

"Is this a bad time?" I asked after she picked up.

She drew in a deep breath and the groaning sounds of springs in a couch drifted through the phone. "No, it isn't. What's up?"

"I got some info from a friend of mine at the hospital."

"What did you learn?"

Not the best news. "Patty Hall is a patient of the state, and so far she's been moving in the slow-cranking system we call public healthcare."

I almost felt her grimace before she spoke. "Ugh. *Fuck.* She probably had to wait for surgery."

I sat down in my seat. "How are you feeling?"

"A bit tired."

Tired from seeing her mom, or maybe she was tired from working too hard. After a bit of digging I'd learned a lot about her condition. The need to confront Carlie about keeping secrets circled my tongue, but she'd been through enough today. At least a few boundaries had been broken between us.

"Have you eaten?" I finally asked.

"I will when I get hungry. I kinda let my fridge end up on E."

I immediately headed to my laptop on my desk nearby. In seconds, I had her address. Next, I shot off a text to Butts. Knowing him, he'd have what I needed in record time. "You shouldn't skip meals."

She laughed a bit. "I never skipped meals when I was with you, did I?"

I was already out the door by the time she finished her

question. She continued chatting as I descended in the elevator.

"Do you remember the time we ate pizza on the curb before I went back to boarding school in Europe?" I asked.

Her voice softened. "Yeah, I do."

"I still go back to Tony's every once in a while for a slice of cheese with anchovies and pepperoni."

She made a rude noise, but her voice was relaxed as I reached the garage where my private car was waiting.

"You hated every bite of that pizza," she remarked.

"But I still ate it anyway. I liked the company and not the food." I still remembered seeing her take bites of that cardboard like pizza, a joyous look on her face. I smiled at the thought. It was me and her that day. Not anyone else. Just another day when our lives would diverge.

"True," she whispered.

My phone shook with a new text: *desired order ready. go to charles and revere st.*

I glanced at my watch. Roland Butts was a ninja.

Carlie and I continued our conversation as the car drove to my first destination. Once the car arrived at the address Butts gave me, a man wearing a white apron ran to my window and passed me a sack. Damn, the contents smelled good. I had yet to eat myself.

Carlie chatted away, unaware of my actions. "Anybody can eat Subway. They are just another sandwich shop."

I rolled my eyes. Not too far for me to go to reach her. "Says the woman who put down a foot-long like nobody's business."

"I have taste, though," she replied. "Subway sandwiches are good and all, but if you want a real sandwich you go to a bakery that specializes in meats."

"You're a New Yorker through and through."

She giggled a bit, I loved hearing that noise.

"You can't take the NY out of me," she added.

"You even used to have an accent."

"I still have one."

"Not really. I can't tell."

She sounded insulted. And a bit more tired. I needed to hurry. By the time my car pulled up to her business suites hotel, she was yawning into the phone.

"You still have your accent," she said softly.

"That I do, Gingerbread."

"Why do you still call me that?"

"Because I like to hear your reaction." I was through the glass doorway into the lobby. A few more footsteps and I'd be at her doorway.

"Where are you? Heading home?" she asked.

"Yeah. I had paperwork to do. I'm thinking I should have some hot leftovers and get some sleep."

She snorted. "Tomas Goodfellow eats leftovers?"

I was walking down her hallway now. The lightness in my feet increased with each step.

"Every now and then yes. My housekeeper and cook do take days off."

"And that's when you should order room service. I sure as hell would."

I briefly muted the phone and knocked hard on her door.

"Who the *fuck* would bother me at a time like this?" she muttered.

I tried not to laugh. *Why ruin the moment?*

"Do your neighbors usually bother you?" I asked after I turned the mute off.

"Just a minute. Somebody is probably complaining about my alarm clocks again."

When she opened the door and saw me, her mouth

dropped open. She looked from her cellphone to the door. *"Wah?"*

"Hey, Gingerbread." Pleased with my successful arrival, I slid around her and came inside. The place was small, just like all business suites these days. All she had was a small kitchenette table for two, so I put the sack down there.

"What are you . . . ?" A smile broke out on her face, revealing her dimple. She was wearing the same clothes from earlier today. Her straight blonde hair hung in messy waves past her shoulders. She was absolutely beautiful.

"Surprise?" I added.

She glanced around her place, and quickly stuffed discarded clothing under a pillow. As she placed papers and such into piles I realized something: I'd never seen her home before. Even when we were younger back in NYC, we always met in public to hang out, or she followed me around. Not once, even when we were intimate in the past, had I visited her.

"You don't want to see my dump," she used to say. *"Shit, I don't even want to see it."* Back then, she shrugged it off, but I knew she was ashamed of what she had compared to me so I never pushed the issue.

"You said you hadn't eaten so I brought you some food," I said.

"Thanks, but you didn't have to . . ." She glanced at the bag longingly. She probably smelled what I did: fresh bread.

As tempted as I was to buy gluten-free bread that would have revealed I knew about her little secret. I ignored her frozen expression and headed to the kitchenette. She didn't say anything when I checked the cupboards and pulled out a few dishes and silverware.

All of this wasn't a big deal and I wanted her to feel that way.

"Looks like you've never used these," I remarked.

"I was never much of a cook."

"I remember that."

"What did you bring?" she asked me.

"You'll see."

I arranged our meal, retrieving her salad first. "A cranberry mango millet salad for you. Full of all sorts of vitamins and minerals to get you ready for work tomorrow. And to show I'm not an ogre, I added a Greek yogurt parfait for dessert."

Her grin was adorable.

I continued. "For me, a rye pastrami sandwich filled with stuff I shouldn't be eating without a warning label."

I added two small servings of loaded baked potato soup. She finally sprung into action when I poured two glasses of water for us.

"This looks delicious." She sat down, not quickly, but slowly as she assessed everything.

"You look dumbfounded."

"I wasn't expecting any of this." She took a bite of her salad and paused to moan. "This is divine." She looked at the bag. "Where did you get this?"

"From one of the chefs at the hotel. He hooks me up every once in a while when I work a long night."

She ran her spoon through the soup a few times, as if she was looking for something. Maybe some ingredients that might hint there was gluten inside. I was ready for that, though.

I added, "I promise there aren't any bugs in there. I didn't have much time since I had you on the phone. The chef happened to have a canceled order from a customer who had dietary restrictions so he gave me a part of their order and threw together a sandwich." I made a face to show I was sorry. "I'd do McDonald's, but the drive-through would have given me away."

I changed my voice to sound like it came through a drive-through speaker. "Welcome to McDonald's. Can I take your order?"

She laughed. "I'd pay money to see you take that Maserati through a drive-through."

I chuckled. "I happen to love Popeyes chicken, just like everyone else."

"You're one of the richest guys in the world, and you don't send a lackey to buy you a bucket of chicken?"

"Not when my arms and legs work just fine." Now that we were past that hump, I sat and watched her eat. Seeing her relaxed and happy was always something I enjoyed. Carlie never took the little things for granted. She always tried everything, even food she didn't recognize, but this time, just knowing she felt uneasy about food bothered me.

She tentatively took a sip of the potato soup. "This is so creamy. Your chef friend is talented."

"That he is."

Carlie made short work of her food. Before she could try to clear our dishes, I took them away and scraped off plates. While I was in the kitchen, I opened the fridge and confirmed my suspicions. Most of the food was gone. She had a few plastic bins of veggies and fruit, but they were pretty empty.

"What are you doing?" she asked.

"Just putting the extra potato soup away. Fresh food is good for the soul. Especially after a long day."

She stood in what could be called her living room and office, her arms wrapped around her shoulders. Was she waiting for me to leave again? Like I always did?

"Aren't you tired?" I finally asked, shoving my hands into my pockets.

"Yeah." She still didn't move.

"So why don't you go to bed?"

"I feel pretty gross, but I haven't found the energy to take care of that."

She remained where she was until I took her hand and led her toward the bedroom. "Tomas . . ." she began, but stopped when we ended up in the connected bathroom.

I leaned over the tub and started running a hot bath.

"I can do it myself," she said.

"Yes, you could, but not tonight."

In minutes, the hot bath was ready. Steam and the smell of peachy soap filled the air. At my side, she'd crossed her arms, but I uncrossed them. "Behave, Gingerbread."

"I'm starting to hate that nickname."

I touched her hairline where a hint of stark red hair grew. "It's fitting. It will be soon anyway."

She let me discard her blouse. I took things slow, my movements unhurried or driven by pleasure. Not that I didn't enjoy unsnapping her bra or exposing her beautiful breasts to my eyes only, but I wanted her to feel safe and relaxed tonight.

She didn't say a word, only taking in the brown-tiled floor while I took off her skirt and removed her panties. Once she was naked before me, I offered a hand to help her into the tub.

"Thank you." She sank into the water and I had to hold myself in check to keep myself from drinking in the delicious curve of her back. The freckles were there as I remembered, this time no longer covered with makeup.

I wanted to draw my lips along her shoulder blades. Instead I waited for her to dip into the water. She hissed and murmured, "This feels wonderful."

I took a seat on the nearby toilet. "Seems like you never take baths."

"Oh, I do. Whenever I get the chance." She leaned back and steam rose from the water. Her breasts emerged from the surface, the pretty nipples with golden rings damp and enticing. I focused on her face.

She continued, her voice content. "Before I started working at your hotel, I used to take a bath every day. I had this massive jet tub with all the bells and whistles." She stretched her arms out to show how wide. "But that huge tub is nothing compared this tiny one with you sitting here with me," she admitted.

I leaned toward her and drew a strand of hair out of her face. She looked at me, and what little resolve I had to not touch her chipped away.

"You're so fucking gorgeous," I breathed.

I ran my hand down the curve of her neck, waiting for her to say something, but she didn't. Her rosy cheeks actually blushed when the tips of my fingers brushed against her collarbone. That blush deepened when I circled the sensitive circle of skin around her pert nipples. The water was warm and I wanted to join her—even if there wasn't enough room for us to bathe together.

Her head tilted to the side and sunk into the tub a bit more as I caressed her skin. My strokes were slow at first, lazy and calm, but soon enough her chest rose to meet my hand. Her lips parted and her tongue snuck out to lick that lower lip. Damn, she was sexy.

Her knees rose out of the water and her legs parted. "Tomas . . ."

Her eyes looked tired, but when I withdrew a bit she snatched my hand. With a lazy smile, she pulled my hand southward into the water. Down her smooth stomach until I reached the silky heat of her channel. She called my name again when I drew my hand upward along her heated flesh. She wouldn't let my arm go, urging me to stroke faster and faster. Deftly with her right hand she held me, while she guided my right hand with her left.

I already knew what pleased her, but letting her control my movements was just as erotic. Especially when she pushed my fingers into her and drew them up to her mouth to lick them. I was closer to her now, unable to control myself. I dipped to flick my tongue along her nipples. Hearing her moans drove me further until she climaxed against my hand.

I was rather wet at this point.

"Sorry about that," she said softly. Her face was glowing. I loved seeing her like this. If I could see her like this every night I would.

"You're not sorry," I chided. "Not in the least bit."

"No, I'm not."

I let her soak for a bit longer, and then I brought a towel to dry her off.

She was quiet as I followed her to bed.

"I need to set my alarms or I'll never wake up," she said. "I'm so exhausted."

"Don't worry, just get some rest."

I got to work setting her alarms like she wanted.

I waited for her to ask me to stay, but she fell asleep instead. I waited for dawn to come and then I left.

Chapter Twenty-One

Carlie

Day after day I used my lunch break to visit the hospital. At first, the nursing staff was a bit put off by me, but they quickly understood I was Patty's daughter and I wasn't leaving until my birth mom woke up.

The first day I came I was surprised to see my mom was in a new room. A private room on the same floor.

A quick text to Tomas confirmed he'd paid for the luxury private room, as well as specialists who checked on my birth mom during the lunchtime rounds. I had a feeling Goodfellow would live up to his surname. Just another debt I couldn't pay. She'd been moved, so there was nothing I could do but be grateful.

Time passed. By the fourth day, it was nice seeing her face, even if she wasn't awake.

By the fifth day, when she did wake up, she opened her mouth and everything changed. "Who the hell are you?"

After twenty-five years apart that was the first thing she said to me. *How lovely.*

"Hi, I'm Carlie . . ." Instead of standing next to her, like I always did, I added some space between us.

"I don't know any *Carlie*." Her voice was hoarse and sleep touched her eyelids.

"I'm . . . your daughter. The one you gave up a long time ago."

Now that made her pause. Her gaze flicked back and forth and she worked her mouth as if by habit.

The awkward moment lingered for so long I wanted to say something to end it.

"What do you want?" Mom finally asked.

"To meet you. I've always wanted to know who you were—"

"Did I ask for you to come find me?" she interrupted.

"No, but—"

"Then you shouldn't be here." She grimaced.

"Are you in pain?" I looked for the call nurse button. "Do you want some medication?"

"Carol, you can leave."

"It's Carlie."

"Whatever your name is, I don't want you here. I specifically asked for no visitors."

"I'm not a visitor."

She harrumphed. In the exact manner I did. "So you're *family* now?"

Hearing those words hurt, but I ignored her jab. I'd waited for this so long a few words from her didn't mean shit compared to what I'd heard on the streets.

"Apparently I'm the only family you've got now. I heard my dad is dead."

She made a noncommittal sound. "Pretty much. He smoked enough cigarettes to earn a free lung disease ticket." Then she turned a bit, only to stop with a grimace and reach for her abdomen.

"You shouldn't move." Hearing her say that about him kicked me in the gut, but I'd deal with that later.

"After Frank died I was so angry about him leaving me alone. Look at me now. Damn karma is an evil bitch with steel-toe boots."

At that moment, a nurse finally came in to check on her. "How are you feeling, Patty?"

"Like week-old shit left on the cement to dry."

The nurse chuckled. "Watch your language, hon."

"When you give me some drugs to feel better, we can talk about my language."

"Have you been keeping your daughter company?" the nurse asked.

"I don't know who this person is. I have *strict* rules about visitors."

The nurse flashed me a look of sympathy, but even I knew Mom could kick me out.

"Talking to others is healthy," the nurse said. "You're about to hit a rough patch until we know your bowels are working properly."

My birth mom frowned and she slowly rubbed her scarf-covered head. "How long until I can eat? I hate this tube running down my throat."

"Hopefully another day or two. We need to keep your stomach from getting distended."

She made a rude sound of utter distaste. "So all I get is that IV?"

"We talked about this before your procedure, Patty," the nurse continued to check her vitals. "This is the plan."

"I didn't plan on waking up ready to eat a horse and the barn it sleeps in."

The nurse patted her on the shoulder. When the nurse

left, I was alone with Patty again. Her lowered eyebrows and frown told me I wasn't welcome.

"Would you like for me to turn on the TV?" I found the remote and turned on the television. This fancier room seemed to have everything. Even a nice couch for family to sleep on.

"Turn it off," she snapped. "If I wanted it on, I would've done it myself."

Keep smiling, Carlie.

Reading people was what I did for a living, which meant I knew for a fact I was trying to swim toward a sinking ship. She was likely hungry and tired. Hungry and tired people lashed out at anyone within striking distance.

And I had a damn target duct-taped to my forehead.

"You need to leave," Mom said again.

I nodded. "I'll be back later then, after you've rested."

"Don't bother."

"I promise I won't be a nuisance. Once you're feeling better you'll want company."

"What makes you think I want to see you *ever* again?" The harsh look on her face felt like a smack on mine. "There was a *reason* why I left you behind."

And with that, I exited stage right.

Chapter Twenty-Two

Tomas

Having Carlie all to myself was something I never thought I could experience. Revealing what happened to my mother was something I never told anyone.

For the Pereira family, my mother's death was like she simply left the family and never came back.

"O que acontece na família Pereira fica na família," Aunt Lucia always said.

What happens in the Pereira family stays in the family.

Getting lost in my thoughts was easy while I waited for Carlie on a bench outside of the hospital. Visiting hours would be over soon. As much as she grumbled about me showing up randomly, being there for her was something I wanted to do, but hospitals like this one still reminded me of the one Saul snuck me into over fifteen years ago.

The London Clinic, just like this hospital, was surrounded by busy streets and nestled deep in the heart of a metropolitan city. On that particular day though, the

London paparazzi wanted a picture of a grieving Good-fellow family member after their tragic loss.

Not only were hospitals for the living, but the dead, as well. I walked in without a mother and I was in the same condition when I left the next morning. My aunts were in transit from overseas and I had no one. Not even my father.

Carlie deserved to have *someone* waiting for her.

I'd waited to see if any of her friends showed up, but they didn't. I shouldn't have been surprised, though. Carlie's independent streak was one of the reasons I loved her. I had a driving need to possess and protect a woman who didn't need me.

I sucked in a deep breath. Did she think of me that way? The one frustrating thing about her was how I always felt like she drew me into her world, chewed me up, and then spit me out.

But I was just as guilty. At first, life had pulled us apart, but now that we were older, we ran away until we were free again.

I waited quietly on the bench until she walked up to me. She didn't say much, merely standing there with her blonde hair pulled back into a messy ponytail and work jacket slung over one arm.

Just like the day before, my Maserati pulled up to the curb to give us a ride to her place, but she paused before getting in.

"You okay?" I asked.

"I don't want to go home," she murmured. "Just take me to your place."

Did she need comfort, or was tonight another meet and fuck?

There wasn't lust shining in her olive green eyes this

time, but something else. Fatigue touched the corners of her mouth. "Just for tonight, Tomas."

I nodded and gave in because I wanted to be with her. When Carlie asked me, I had trouble refusing her, but this was a road we'd been down before. All the fucking led to one place: someone's bed.

Instead of eating the dinner I offered, she went straight to my bedroom. Naturally, I followed. Once past the double doors, her heels were silent on the carpeted floor. The room was dim—the only light filtered through the opened curtains along the floor-to-ceiling windows. Shadows enveloped her curves. Her clothes whispered as they shrugged off her shoulders. I watched her place her jacket and skirt in a neat pile on the nightstand.

Just walk out, Tomas. Let her rest.

Moonlight hit her back as she unsnapped her black bra and discarded her lacy panties.

Tension descended from my stomach to my groin. Did she know had easily she threw me off kilter?

She slipped into bed and pushed back the covers on the other side of the king-sized bed: her invitation. She didn't want to sleep.

I crossed the room in a few strides. My clothes came off soon after.

Now we were in bed together again, lying face-to-face, and she waited. I cupped her cheek and enjoyed the smoothness of her skin. Her gaze was cast downward, a slight smile to her lips. She was waiting for me to act. For me to do as I pleased. What I wanted utmost though, I couldn't have.

We tortured ourselves every time we did this, and yet, we gravitated to face each other as if we trusted ourselves. Damn, I wanted to brush my lips against hers. To feel her tremble underneath me as I kissed her. She blinked, her eyes searching mine. Her breath had quickened and her pulse thrummed against my palm.

"Carlie . . ." My voice had a dark edge.

Kiss me right now. The command lingered on my tongue, but I refused to say it.

She turned away from me. I pulled her back against my chest and inhaled the scent of her hair. That delicate pear scent drew me in every single time. The curve of our bodies fit together perfectly. All my hard lines against her soft ones. I couldn't resist the pulse of my hips toward her ass. I hungered for her and she responded in kind, grinding her ass against my hardening length.

If she wouldn't let me kiss her lips, I'd kiss her elsewhere.

I kissed her shoulder first. A lingering brush of my lips along her shoulder blade. From there, I traveled down her back. A lick here, a feather-like tongue trail there. She shivered with each stroke.

I'd lay claim to the places that belonged to me. She was mine to sample. Mine to taste. I licked her hips and turned her over to touch the places I'd been aching to caress: her long legs to the curve of her ass. She tried to reach for me.

"Do I have to tie you up?" I warned her with a growl.

"Yes." My little treasure was still defiant.

"Yes, *what*?" My bed. My rules.

"Yes, sir." She sucked in a breath. "I need you."

"No." She wasn't getting her way tonight. In a drawer beside my bed I had enough bondage hemp to tie her up until she couldn't so much as twitch. If I wanted I could punish her until she climaxed from my hand alone.

But tonight I was getting what *I* wanted: to give her pleasure in the manner I see fit.

With one hand I held her wrists above her head, and

with the other I gripped her hip as my tongue traced a circle around her pink areola. *"Bela."*

I sucked and nipped, drawing her deep into my mouth. Every moan and soft sound she made drove me crazy. The need to bury myself inside of her grew painful.

"I want to hear you come over and over again," I told her in Portuguese as I descended along her stomach. I let go of her hands. "Stay still. I want to feel you tremble while I fuck you with my mouth."

She quivered as my nose brushed against her belly button. I settled between her legs, eager to sample her swollen flesh. All it took was a long lick of my tongue from her clit to her pussy and she bucked hard. I came at her again, latching onto her sweet bud. This was the place where I wanted to be, feeling her squirm while my tongue darted incessantly into her wet heat.

"Tomas!" she gasped.

As expected, Carlie didn't behave for very long. As much I enjoyed feeling her hands caress me, I wasn't bending to her whims tonight.

So I froze and then I got up. She watched me the whole time. In the silence of the bedroom, the only sound was of her contracted breaths and finally her groan of frustration. The need to punish her filled my senses, but spanking her or using the flogger wouldn't get my point across.

I stared at her beautiful body. Her legs were still parted and her pert nipples begged me to touch them, but I didn't move until she looked away. A small surrender on her part.

Now that she was complacent, I returned to the bed and settled my face between her legs.

"What are you going to do, *Coraçao*?" I finally asked.

She shuddered from each exhale I made along her clit.

Her hands hovered over my head then she slowly placed them above hers. "I'm going to do as you please."

"That's my girl." Relentless, I sampled every part of her until she screamed my name again and again. Tonight was about the pleasure I wanted to give her.

Now that she was sated and running her fingers along my chest, I still hungered for something more. And it wasn't just kissing her. Every single time I waited for her outside of the hospital, I hoped she'd want more. Perhaps we'd find that bliss we had before I left for Europe all those years ago.

I hoped she'd stay, but the moment she drifted off, she was ready to leave.

If I kept doing this to myself, I'd never be able to let her go without hurting both of us.

Carlie

All these years, I wondered where my stubborn streak came from.

"Ms. Hall, do you have arrangements for aftercare?" the discharge nurse asked.

"I don't need—"

"Yes, she does." I stepped forward.

Over the past two weeks, my birth mom managed to progress from the point where they removed her feeding tube up until she could eat. Now that she was ready to go home, I was here to make sure she got there safely. *Whether she wanted my help or not.*

"Why do you keep doing this?" she implored.

"Because you're my mother." I wheeled her out of the hospital and helped her into my rental car.

"I don't have any money," she grumbled as she got into the Camry's front seat.

"That's apparent. I already paid for the car for the week."

"Don't expect much," she finally said. And that was when I knew she'd at least be quiet for a while.

Until I got her address from Tomas this morning, I had no idea where she lived or if she had a place to stay. All I knew was that I had time off and I planned to use it . . . for her.

The ride towards the southwest was silent for over forty minutes until we pulled up to a quiet west Boston neighborhood. I'd never been to this area before. We were quite far from downtown—beyond the skyscrapers and busy sidewalks. This neighborhood seemed more countryside than cityscape.

All the houses along this street were smaller cottages with brick and wood façades. I spotted my mom's home right away: the lawn, with patches of brown dirt intermingled with overgrown grass, hadn't been mowed in months.

"Here we are. Wayland," I said.

We weren't technically in Boston anymore.

Mom stayed in the front seat since she didn't have any suitcases. She'd apparently worn her clothes to the procedure so she now wore them home.

At first, I thought she'd walk right up to the house and leave me behind to lock her door, but instead, she leaned against the door with a painful grimace.

"Here." I offered my hand since I knew she hated anyone touching her torso.

Slowly, she got out of the car. A sheen of sweat lined her brow already. She'd pushed herself to reach this far. Her feet took each step one at a time up to the house. I stood closely behind her, ready to catch her. By the time we reached the door, I wished I would've rented a wheelchair.

Her face was ashen as she reached into her purse and I waited patiently. The need to ask her for the keys kicked me hard, but if she was as stubborn as I was, she didn't want any help.

And then she dropped the keys.

"Well, fuck," she blurted.

As deftly as I could without seeming helpful, I bent over and picked them up. I placed them on my palm as if she was picking them up from the ground.

She didn't say thanks either, merely unlocked the door and ambled inside.

Since the outside wasn't that big, I wasn't expecting a mansion, but this place felt cramped and stuffy. We walked into an open living room and kitchen. To my left, the living room's two windows were drawn shut with yellow, pink, and black curtains. Dust blanketed the air. Her furniture was nondescript, like the kind you'd find at a garage sale.

Patty ambled to the nearest spot to sit, her dining room table. The table was covered in papers, a box of cereal, and various VHS tapes. A bunch of John Hughes movies sat on the top.

At least she had good taste in movies.

"Need some water?" I asked her.

She was breathing pretty hard. According to the nurse though, she wouldn't be due for another dose of pain meds until this afternoon. She'd have to hold out for a while.

"Yeah." She pointed to her right toward the kitchenette.

I left my purse on the couch and headed into the dim kitchen. Finding a light switch turned into a game of hunt and peck until I spotted it behind a dusty bread box with a stack of small boxes on top. There were papers all over the counters and the dirty dishes overflowed in the sink.

I frowned and my stomach sank. She'd lived by herself in this mess while going to chemotherapy every week.

"There might not be any clean cups," she admitted. "Just rinse it out."

She tried not to sound embarrassed, but behind her gruff manner, even I could see it.

"These two don't look too bad." I held the only two glasses that didn't have food crusted on them or matter growing along the edges. I filled a cup with cold water and gave it to her.

She took a long drink. "Thanks," she mumbled.

"Sure thing." I hadn't called her "Mom" since we'd left the hospital. Calling her that only pissed her off. Since we'd come to a bit of a truce, I didn't want to be the first one to open fire.

For a moment I stood in the middle of the room and I wasn't sure what to do next. Of course, my apartment wasn't the most perfect of spaces, but I had housekeeping service and they vacuumed and dusted once a week.

My eyes scanned from the old food containers on the coffee table to the mountain of papers under the kitchen table. *Damn, this is bad.* What about the places I hadn't checked yet like the bathroom or the fridge?

One step at a time.

I shrugged off my running shoes and left them near the door.

First, things first, I needed to get her comfortable.

Initially, she didn't want to move, but finally, with my help I walked with her through the hallway to her bedroom. I ignored the messiness in that room, too. We walked over dirty clothes, past a few piles of cozy mystery novels, and then to the queen-sized bed.

Her covers didn't smell clean.

All this time my mom hadn't lived in a mansion like my fantasies or a quiet house with my dad where she baked cookies like Betty Crocker.

She'd lived like this battling cancer.

I blinked rapidly, trying to clear my head before I lost it.

"Get some sleep, Mo—Patty," I began. "I'll see about some warm soup for lunch."

Mom mumbled a bit, but she drifted off not long after hitting the sheets.

I glanced around the room before forcing myself to leave. I had so much work to do. I tried to close the door after myself and failed—there was too much stuff. I gave up and left. Down the hall from her bedroom was the bathroom. That room wasn't too bad. The sink was covered in old toothpaste and soap scum. Towels had been used over and over again and smelled musty.

At the far end of the hallway was a pretty big storage room with the furnace and water heater. Boxes and such had been crammed into every space available.

So that was it. The place where my mom had lived all this time.

Reality dropped into my lap with a heavy thud.

NOT LONG AFTER Mom fell asleep, I was left alone in a house that threatened to suffocate me.

I missed Tomas, too.

Since it was evening time in the UK, I placed a phone call to check on my business there. Everything was running smoothly. Of course, I smiled and nodded at the appropriate times, not really wanting to hear about the parties

I'd missed or the networking opportunities that had slipped through my fingers.

This was the place I was needed the most.

Standing around wouldn't fix the current situation so I took things one step at a time over the afternoon. I opened every window that could be opened, most were painted shut. I grabbed a trash bag and threw away TV dinner containers. She didn't have dish soap or a dishwasher so I made a trip to the local discount store and foraged for supplies. Goods in hand, I managed to do the dishes and clear space on the stove so I could warm up some beef broth.

When I opened the door to her fridge, I was prepared for a mess, but what I didn't expect to find was a bunch of boxed meals with the words "gluten free" on the sides. Her loaf of bread, which wasn't recognizable as bread at this point, was also gluten free.

I scanned what little perishable goods she had in the cabinets and found more of the same.

Oh fuck.

I shouldn't have been surprised, and yet I was. All of the gluten-free food was expired, though. She hadn't eaten any of it. I cleared out the old food and added the food I bought.

"Fresh food is good for the soul," Tomas had said. "Especially after a long day." He was right.

A bit of sunshine streamed into the house and revealed the cobwebs in the corners, but the cozy home came alive a bit. I wished Tomas could see how much I'd accomplished.

I was about to check on Mom when the man on my mind texted me: *You're not home, are you all right?*

Had he stopped by my hotel again with a meal? I grinned briefly, but my smile faded away as I poured some of Mom's soup into a bowl. The food he'd brought me last time . . . I tried to recall every single thing he'd pulled out of that bag. That night I'd craved normalcy and he'd presented a miracle, but none of the food he'd given me had gluten in it.

My throat stuck mid-swallow. *Did he know?*

He couldn't. That wasn't Tomas. He would've confronted me about it.

I texted back: *I'm at Mom's house. It's a hot mess. I will drive back tonight.*

Need me? he replied.

I gripped the cellphone tighter.

Just type yes, I thought.

I bit my lower lip.

Oh how I wanted to type back yes, but I typed, *I'm good,* instead.

I had to handle this on my own. If Tomas got involved, I'd be deeper in his debt.

I drove back to Mom's place every day after work for the rest of the week. After that, we settled into a rhythm for the next two weeks. When she wasn't complaining, she was actually calmer.

"Where did you put my medication?" she asked from the bathroom.

"It's in the *medicine* cabinet—where it belongs."

"I leave everything on the counter so I *see* it in the morning."

"The bottles were covered in toothpaste." I was busy making her dinner. It seemed like she was doing well with the broth. So far the bowls were empty when I came the next day.

"This is where I brush my teeth, you know," she griped.

I laughed. "Are you having a toothbrush party?" I left

the food on the now cleared kitchen table and went to check on her.

She was standing in front of the mirror, clad in a ratty bathrobe, and her scarf was off. A bit of reddish peach fuzz covered the top of her head. My heart lurched at the sight. She'd lost so much to cancer. I kept my gaze to her face.

My throat grew dry as my stomach hollowed out. Why couldn't I have met her before she was like this? As I took in the lines next to her eyes, and the moles along her neck, I tried to imagine what she'd looked like when she was younger. Had she looked like me? My birth mom's eyes still flashed with a spark of rebellion, but time sure had made her grumpy.

"Leave my medicine alone." She pointed at the meager counter space. "You're messing everything up."

"No problem. Come eat."

"I'll come when I'm good and ready."

"Then get ready faster or the broth will be cold."

She could throw any barbs she liked. I was far better.

"Who was the lady who knocked on my door yesterday?" Mom asked when she sat down at the table.

"Did she come around one?"

"I dunno. She kept babbling about how she was here to tidy up the place."

"Oh, that was from the maid service I called. She was supposed to pick up and make you some lunch."

Mom tsked. "I don't need any strangers coming in here and messing up my things. You already do a bang-up job of that."

"Of course I do. Like when I killed that massive spider creeping around your bathroom."

"Now that was a mercy killing. I'll give you kudos for that one."

I snorted. "Thanks?"

A hint of a devilish grin touched her lips, and I couldn't resist smiling in return while I watched her eat the broth. Every time she bent over though, she cringed a bit.

"Have you taken your pain meds yet?" I asked.

"Yeah, I took some this morning, but I need—"

I slipped her another dose. The label on the bottle said she could have at least six today.

"Thanks," she mumbled.

"When do you need to see the doctor for a follow-up?"

"I don't remember," she admitted. Fatigue pressed into her features.

"I'll call Dr. Craft and find out."

She only nodded.

I washed the dishes and touched a small landscape painting on the wall. "When did you move into this house? This is a nice neighborhood."

She slurped her soup. "After Frank died I traveled like I used to do when I was younger. After he passed, I ended up here. The area had fewer properties back then. Now a bunch of liberals are taking over."

I had to laugh at that remark. She did get a bunch of mail from the local Democrats. She was probably hiding a liberal inside of her. She was far from conservative.

"Where did you go when you were younger?" Prying was hard not to do, and bit by bit I tried to draw things out of her.

"All over the place. Mostly small towns with the band."

I turned to look at her. "You *played* in a band?"

"Oh, no! I was a groupie who sort of graduated into becoming the band manager. That's how I met Frank."

I held my tongue and waited for her to keep going.

"Back in the late eighties, traveling was so much more fun compared to today. Of course, when our truck died, we couldn't perform, but we had a blast seeing the countryside. Now folks get on a computer and they can see shit which used to be a speck on a map."

"That's true." I wanted to ask so badly why there weren't any photos of her or my dad around the house. I wished I could've seen what she looked like when she was younger. Even more questions swam around my head: What about my grandparents? Did my mom have a good childhood?

Instead of asking what I really wanted to know, I asked a question I knew she wouldn't mind answering.

"What was the band called?" I asked.

"Rutger Rose. Not my idea."

"Not bad. Not badass, but not bad."

"They weren't too bad. The lead singer, Dan, had some real nice pipes. A nice ass, too."

"I think most hair bands in the eighties required tight pants and a nice ass. What about the other band members?" Yep, I could be sly when I tried.

"There was Quincy on keyboards—I had to move heaven and earth to keep him with us. He hated all the smaller gigs we had. Aaron was on the drums, and my Frank played bass."

"A decent size." I could imagine my mom, around my age, traveling around with a band. My heart sank a bit. Had she chosen that life instead of taking care of me?

Instead of letting my thoughts fester, I grabbed my phone, searched the band name on the Internet, and found a few hits. Including some pictures.

"Is this the band?" I asked.

I showed her an image of four guys, most of them thin and wearing enough guy liner to put a makeup artist out of business.

"Oh, yeah." A smile really brightened her face. "That

tall guy in the front with purple leather is Dan, the black guy is Quincy, and the short guy in the back is Aaron. The guy on the left is my Frank."

She took the phone from me when I backed up. She stared at the picture for a bit. I was just as transfixed on the man who was my father. Before I only had a name and I knew he was dead. Now I had a picture.

"I can't believe some dumbass made a fan page." She scrolled down the page. "They never played at venues bigger than a few hundred people."

So they never made it big. *How sad.*

"Oh wow, this is *old*." I glanced over her shoulder and saw a woman with beautiful curly, red hair. She sat on the back of a truck with band equipment all around her. Her crop top and hair-sprayed locks screamed eighties, but she was gorgeous by any standard.

"That's you," I whispered.

"I didn't think anyone would have this picture." Her voice grew quiet. "I could barely run a comb through that thing."

I couldn't either, which was why I had my hair pressed, but looking at the glow in her eyes and the way she smiled at the camera made me smile, too. I waited for her to say more, but she piped up. Maybe she was remembering better times. Old photos did that to me, too. Sophie had kept a few pics from when we lived in our old apartment in NYC. Every time I saw them though, I never saw our exuberant faces—I only recalled how hard we had to work to pay the rent and scrape together money for food.

Our youth should've been a golden time in our lives. The reality was far bleaker.

"Do you want more broth?" I finally asked.

"Naw, I'm good." She got up and headed back to the bathroom.

I used the time to clean up her room and then moved into the kitchen, but when she left the bathroom, she went into the bedroom and didn't come back out again.

At least, she'd opened up a bit.

∾

THE NEXT DAY, I couldn't shake the image of my mother standing on the back of that truck, the light shining on her red hair. All day at work the Rutger Rose fan page distracted me. They were nothing more than a bar rock band that never hit it big, but it was my mom's image that stayed with me.

By the end of the day, I couldn't take it anymore.

The salon in the hotel was booked solid for the rest of the month, but one of the ladies took pity on me when she saw my hairline.

"You work at the concierge desk, right?" one of the hair stylists asked.

"Yeah, I'm the assistant chef concierge."

She made a face and touched my hairline. "You can't go out like that, girl."

Since I had yet to make time to get my hair handled, I'd been wearing a headband. Apparently, I had forgotten it today, which meant I'd spent most of the day flashing horrible hair. The straight to frizzy had to be ghastly.

"Come back in an hour," the stylist declared. "I'll work on two people at once."

So I came back in an hour, ready to do something I hadn't done in a long time: I was going back to my natural hair color.

The stylist was busy, as she'd told me, but one of the assistants washed my hair first.

Next came the hard part. My hair had been dyed

blond and straightened, which meant a longer dying time. As I sat in the chair, I hoped my mom would remember to eat dinner.

The temptation to call on her to check the house was there, but she likely wouldn't answer the phone. When I was there, she never answered the phone unless she recognized the number.

Five hours later, my hair hung to my shoulders in thick curls.

"Are you sure you don't want me to press it straighter?" the lady asked.

"Nope, I'm ready for a change," I declared.

When she turned my chair around and I saw myself, I grinned again and again.

My makeup was gone and my cheeks were peppered with freckles. My naked lips stretched into a smile.

This was the Carlie I remembered.

By the time I left the salon, it was late at night. I still called Patty. She didn't answer so I gave in and drove to the house.

Was she all right? In a panic I was mad at myself for not checking up on her.

I arrived to a house in darkness.

The kitchenette was clean and I noticed she hadn't warmed up any food. I peeked in on her. Her lamp was on and she was curled on her side.

"Patty?" I whispered. Her face was in a grimace and she was breathing fast. "Are you all right?"

"I'm fine," she murmured.

"I called the house, but you didn't pick up."

"I didn't feel like getting up."

I guess I was upset for nothing. I chuckled softly. "I can imagine."

I fetched her some medication and water. "Here you go."

She looked at me, blinked and then accepted her medication. "You changed your hair."

"Yeah, I did."

I left her to sleep. Instead of driving back to the city though, I curled up on her couch. Hearing the sounds of her breathing in the other room finally set me at ease. I would've set my alarm clock on my cell, but this time I didn't care.

Chapter Twenty-Three

Tomas

The hotel sale was moving forward smoothly. The two teams from Asia continued to express interest, but neither of them had the type of portfolio I was interested in.

Carlie had been in and out of the hotel and we'd had little time to connect. Keeping myself busy with work seemed the best. Everything I wanted was right in front of me. All I had to do was sell the Goodfellow Tower and move on to the next project.

When I was thinking about Carlie, I'd distract myself with the next sites. So far, potential project locations in London and South Korea had caught my interest.

This was my zone, though. I could focus on numbers, planning, and construction and not think about the woman who was pulling me deeper into her life.

Wendy entered my office with the latest notes from the meeting. "Is there anything else I can do for you today, Mr. Goodfellow?"

I shook my head.

"You've been buried in work for the past few days. Would you like for me to clear your evening so you can relax? Maybe have dinner with that pretty lady I saw you with the other day?"

I never mixed business with pleasure. Women never came to my office. I kept any relationships on the twenty-second floor at best.

I shook my head. "No need to clear my schedule. I have no plans tonight." I truly didn't. Carlie was spending more time with her mother and I would've done the same.

"Understood, Mr. Goodfellow. I'll get you those numbers for the Seoul site then."

I jumped back into my work, ready to move on if necessary.

~

Carlie

As expected, I woke up horrifically late. And in pain, too.

Mom's couch didn't have springs anymore, so my poor back had become one with the bumpy surface. The coils groaned as I turned over. The room was bathed in light—the first sign of my impeding doom—and the house was quiet. Mom hadn't gotten up yet as I'd hoped.

I checked my cellphone and the time was far later than I wanted it to be. As in ten a.m. later.

I rolled off the couch and managed not to fall onto the floor. Rubbing my back didn't reduce the ache from lying there all night.

Instead of hurrying to work though, I went into Patty's room to check on her.

She was in the same position I'd left her in. Curled up on her side. How long had she slept like that?

"Patty?" I approached her, but she didn't move. I got closer until I was practically near enough to hear the slight rise and fall of her breath. Tentatively, I reached out and touched her side. Her skin was warm, but her sour sweat made me wrinkle my nose.

Was she even taking care of herself?

Let the home care person you hired take care of this, I reminded myself. But the lady wouldn't get here until the afternoon and my mom hadn't gotten up in a long time.

I glanced at my watch again. I was already late anyway. It didn't matter. I left the bedroom and got some broth cooking on the stove. While that warmed up, I made a phone call to Mom's doctor. Then I started the shower.

Once I knocked out those tasks, I marched back into the room. "Time to get up, Patty."

By the time I shook her a few times, she muttered and finally stirred. "I'm tired."

"Yeah, I'm tired, too. We partied pretty hard last night."

That got a laugh out of her. "Did we have exotic dancers?"

"Fuck yeah. You slept through the guy with the foot-long dick, though."

"I always miss the big dick ones." I helped her out of bed.

"How's your stomach?" I asked.

"Shitty," she muttered.

"After you shower, we're going to the clinic to get you checked out. I called ahead for a sick visit."

I couldn't see her while she ambled to the bathroom, but I could feel her looking at me. I didn't turn around until she reached the bathroom.

"Do you need help?" I called to her.

"Not unless you plan to help me take a sh—"

"Sounds good, Patty." I shook my head with amusement.

An hour later, I had called in to take another day off, Patty was clean again, and we were on the road back into the city for Mom's doctor appointment. Compared to all the chatter and complaining back at the house, Mom changed the moment we reached the medical center.

She wouldn't look at me, and she fell into a silence as she closed in on herself. Even when I pushed her in the wheelchair to her appointment she didn't whisper a word.

Did she feel the same way about hospitals that I did?

We didn't have to wait long, and soon enough a physician checked her out. I was ready to leave the room, but Patty didn't say anything. I waited for the snide comments even during the checkup. The doctor even tried to joke with her. I tried not to look during the exam, but the length of time he took to check her abdomen bothered me a bit. Her stomach was distended and slightly discolored.

"Is that to be expected post-surgery?" I asked, finally giving in.

"A little discoloration is to be expected." He explained how part of her intestines had to be removed due to the bowel cancer. The cancer she'd likely contracted from a poor diet as someone with celiac disease.

"Have you been taking it easy, Patty?" the doctor asked.

Mom responded with a bunch of one-syllable answers.

I jumped in and responded when she wouldn't. Somebody had to care.

"What about your diet?" he asked.

"I've been managing her meals," I piped in.

"Are you familiar with her new diet?" he asked.

I nodded. "I was recently diagnosed with celiac disease myself."

"Then I'm assuming you're familiar with the diet and potential complications?" he said.

I looked away and he smiled. "You're not the first or the last patient to do that." He marked notes on his chart. "If you have time today, I'd like to schedule time for you and your mom to meet with our staff dietician. It won't take long and she can talk to you about your lifestyle change."

Yes, my new life was a lifestyle change.

"Thanks, Dr. Craft," I said since Mom didn't plan to.

After that, we spent the whole day in the city. From the doctor's appointment to our meeting with the dietician. I learned more from the dietician than I could ever glean from the Internet.

"Just don't read the Internet unless it's from a reputable source," was her first tip. "There's conflicting information all over the place. When in doubt, consult the reading material I gave you. Depending on your condition's severity, as well as your mother's, your problems from malabsorption could be worse due to what you're eating."

Boy, did she have a point there.

After Mom's appointment, we ate lunch downtown at one of the restaurants the dietician recommended. The moment we left the medical center, my mom was back to her old self.

"Do they have anything good here?" she asked.

"Yeah, the steak is marvelous, and I believe Dr. Craft cleared you to eat a few bites."

That got a smile from her. "I hope you know I'm not paying for this meal."

"No, I didn't, Patty." As gruff as she could be, I found I rather liked her bluntness.

She was just like me.

As I watched her eat her lunch, all the while talking unabashedly about the diners around us, I couldn't help thinking about what would happen to her tomorrow. I would eventually have to return to work. Would she get up tomorrow morning?

Quitting quickly came to mind.

You need a job, Carlie. You barely have enough money to take care of yourself. What about your business in the UK?

I could get a part-time job closer to where she lived. I didn't sit long on the decision. I finally had her—even if she was calling the lady across the room a weird-looking hooker.

"Do you even know what a weird-looking hooker wears?" I asked.

"I was the manager of a band," Mom replied. "I've seen hookers, Carlie. Most of them try not to look cheap and they fail."

I rolled my eyes and a decision was made right then and there.

I'd finally found her and leaving her behind to pursue my career wasn't gonna happen.

Warmth filled my chest and the doubts pressing down on my shoulders eased. This was what I wanted.

"Patty, how would you feel about me coming over tomorrow?" I began.

She shrugged and stirred her salad around her plate. "I don't mind."

"What if I stayed longer than tomorrow?"

She looked up at me and I found it hard to read her expression. Did I do the same thing? "You're not that *bad* to be around."

"Oh really, that's good."

"I thought the minute you walked through that hospital door it would be all about how I left you behind. I'll be honest and say it: I chose the road over you, but I did try." She looked away briefly. "For eight months, Frank and I tried to keep you, but we lived on the road with a bunch of grown-ass men and there was no proper place for you to sleep. Having a kid in hotel rooms around a bunch of groupies wasn't good either." She bit her lower lip. "I tried . . ."

I reached out for her hand. I thought she'd pull away, but she let me place my hand over hers. "I always imagined you did."

"You were a horrible baby. You cried all the damn time."

I almost choked on my food. "I believe that's what infants do."

"And you never wanted to stay in one place."

"That, too." Now she was taking things a bit too far.

"What I'm trying to say was giving up my own kid was the hardest thing I'd ever done. I'll be honest, there were times when I hated seeing you waiting for me. Seeing you meant I couldn't be free anymore. If I gave you away I wouldn't worry about you anymore. Out of sight, out of mind."

"I'd wondered about that, too."

Her eyebrows lowered as if she wondered what I meant.

"Does out of sight, out of mind really work, Patty?" I asked softly.

"Not really." Now my mom was crying.

The hard wedge she'd placed between us didn't seem like a mountain to climb anymore.

She wiped her mouth with her napkin. "So what happens now?"

"I make sure you get back on your feet, we eat healthy shit, and you make bad jokes at my expense."

She gave me a devilish grin. "I think I like this plan."

Chapter Twenty-Four

Tomas

After a long workday, I didn't expect to see someone waiting for me beside the Maserati. A woman in a light blue dress with curly red hair stood next to the doors, her arms crossed and a serene look on her face.

A gust of wind blew her red ringlets across her face. Her ruby lips parted and her cheeks blossomed into a smile, revealing that adorable dimple of hers. The light from a streetlamp hit the back of her head and her beauty took my breath away.

"Hey, Goodfellow," she said with a wave.

"Hey, Gingerbread." I crossed the distance between us. "You look absolutely . . ." I tried to find the right words and I failed.

"What are you doing here?" I asked her.

"I came to see you."

I stuffed my hands into my pockets. "Are you all right?"

"I'm much better now."

"You look that way. Do you have time to talk?"

"I've got plenty of time. I was hoping you could clear your schedule for coffee or maybe even dinner. Wishful thinking, but I've had so much happen to me . . ."

"Of course. We should have dinner and a few drinks."

Her smile faltered. "If you don't mind, I was hoping we could grab some food and head back to your place. I'd like some quiet time."

"Anything." But I saw where this was going. Behind closed doors, we'd go through the same motions again, but instead of getting in the car, she took my hand and pulled me down the street.

"Let's go," she urged.

Her warm hand squeezed mine.

"I thought you wanted to grab a bite to eat and head to my place?" I asked.

"We are, but I want to take a walk first, maybe pick up some street food before we head back."

Now this was unusual.

So we strolled down Thirty-Fourth Street.

"Any idea where we're going?" I asked.

She shrugged and the heat from the late summer day touched her face. "No idea. I just . . . missed seeing you. I got spoiled when you brought me lunches all the time."

"Not hard at all. Speaking of the hospital, how is your mom?"

"She takes one day at a time. I'd like to say she's doing better, but I don't know how long it takes to recover from major bowel surgery. I guess she has good days and bad days. More bad ones than good."

I nodded.

On our way around the block, we stopped at a few places. One in particular I wasn't expecting. I even tried to avoid it. "Do you want food from here?"

"I just want to go in."

"I'd rather have a burger," I offered.

"Just c'mon." She browsed the aisle, looking at the cakes and such. She stopped in front of the window. "There is something I've been needing to tell you for a long time."

"What's on your mind?"

She bit her lower lip. "I have celiac disease . . . There I said it." She released a deep breath.

"I knew already."

She released a long sigh. "I had a feeling."

"Why did you wait so long?"

"Fear. I didn't want you to pity me. I've always tried to roll with the punches."

"I've never pitied you."

"Sometimes I forget that." She leaned on the counter to ask the clerk a question. "Do you have any gluten-free options?"

"Sorry, ma'am," the man said, "we don't have anything. Our boss said something about cross-contamination. We prepare all our breads in the kitchen in the back."

She nodded and smiled as if she'd heard that many times before. So we left the bakery.

"I was always wondering how you got that meal for me the night you showed up at my apartment. You knew then too, huh?" she asked.

"Yeah."

"How did you find out?"

He told me about my birthday dinner and I laughed. "So you're the mystery man who paid for our meal."

I intertwined our fingers. Holding her hand felt damn good.

So much time had passed since that night. By the time we picked up some burgers, an hour had passed with just me and her. We hadn't walked around like this in a long time. Maybe she'd be open to doing it more.

Once we returned to the hotel, we rode up my private elevator to my penthouse. Anticipation made it hard for me to concentrate. The need to touch her again rocketed through me, but I wanted to stretch out every moment without hurrying. When the dawn came she'd be gone.

I didn't want to lose a single moment.

We ate our food on the penthouse patio. Between bites we grinned like fools.

"Is it that good?" I asked.

"Hell yeah." She held up how much she had left. She didn't complain while she ate her beef patty wrapped in lettuce.

I couldn't stop staring at her. "Do you remember the first time we kissed?"

That made her pause. "Of course I do." She made a face as if she'd tasted something bad. "You were awful at it." She darted her tongue, in the most unappealing manner, into the opening of her lettuce. "You did *this* over and over again."

I busted out laughing. "I was that bad?"

"You were twenty. Like you knew any better."

I put my burger down and wiped off my hands. "What about now?"

"What do you mean?" She put down her food.

"Don't play coy with me. You know what I'm asking. Have I improved?"

Her olive-green eyes blinked and she glanced away as if suddenly shy. My heart was beating so fast I had trouble catching my breath.

I traced my fingertips over her lips. "You still make my heart race like the first time."

I lightly kissed her forehead and nothing else. Every

part of my being begged for me to trail my mouth along the bridge of her nose to her lips, but I didn't budge.

Your move, Gingerbread.

I waited. Then it came. A brief brush of her lips against mine. The kiss was tentative, just like that summer day when we kissed for the first time. Our heads tilted and I drew her seat closer to mine. We continued to kiss, a sensual dance beginning with our tongues. The wind blew between the buildings, making her hair tickle my face, but nothing would stop me from doing what I'd waited years to do.

Finally, we parted, our breathes quickened and my heart still beating fast enough to cause a dull ache.

I drew her thick hair out of her face, brushing my fingertips against her brown freckles. "Carlie, stay with me tonight."

"Is that an order?" she whispered.

"No."

She tilted her head. "I'll stay."

We left behind our food and laid next to each other on one of the wide lawn chairs. I pulled her close to me and we lay face-to-face, our foreheads a mere hairsbreadth apart. Overwhelmed with emotion, I had to speak.

"I love you, *Coração.*" I kissed her again, lingering long enough to hear her sigh. I'd say those words all night until she knew the depth of my love for her. "I've always loved you."

"I know, Goodfellow. I love you, too."

I closed my eyes, content to sleep a bit knowing she'd be there when I woke up.

AFTER SLEEPING on the lawn chair for an hour, I carried

her back into the penthouse. As nice as the weather was outside, Carlie belonged in my bed.

After spending the night making love to her, I thought I'd be exhausted into the early morning, but when sunlight began to flood the floor-to-ceiling windows in the room, I stirred, reaching out across the bed. I expected to find the space empty like I usually did.

She's still here.

"Carlie," I murmured.

She rolled about and had migrated to the far side of the bed. Even her feet hung off the edge. I gently wrapped my arms around her waist and tugged her back to me. I ran my nose along the back of her head. I was in complete bliss.

She'd stayed.

The warmth of her naked body snuggled against mine made touching her too hard to resist. I caressed her hips from the back of her thighs to the front. My fingertips followed the trail along her waist, to the curve of her breast, and then her shoulders.

We spent the day together in bed. Matter of fact, she even called in sick from my bed. We ordered room service and watched an action flick starring Bruce Willis—her favorite actor.

What mattered was having her beside me, smiling and carefree—until the day was almost over and she began to get dressed.

"Is something wrong?" I asked.

"Yes, I have to go check on my mom."

"I think you both should move in at the hotel. I could get a nurse for her—"

"You're selling the hotel."

"Yes, I am but that shouldn't matter."

"So are you going to drag us around with you from project to project then?"

"It doesn't have to be like that, Carlie. I could make sure both of you are comfortable."

Her frown deepened. "You know that isn't the life I want to lead. If I wanted to be a mistress, I would've signed up to be one from the get-go after I turned eighteen."

"So what are you saying?"

"I'm quitting my job and I'm going to go stay with Mom."

"What about us?" Now I was getting angry even though I didn't want to.

"You're about to leave again, Tomas. We'd drift back to how we were before."

I took her hand before she had a chance to take a step back. "No, we wouldn't. This time is different."

"No, it isn't. We always keep getting pulled apart. You're selling the hotel and I need to be with my mom so she can recover and we can form a relationship again. How can we do both?"

"We'll do it because we love each other." I pressed my forehead against hers like last night. "Isn't that enough?"

"Not right now it isn't."

I opened my mouth to speak, but what could I say. I'd choose my own mother if she were still alive—and yet—I didn't want her to leave again. This whole night was probably her way of saying goodbye and I had to let her be the daughter she always wanted to be.

When Carlie pulled away from me, I let her go and watched her walk away.

Chapter Twenty-Five

Carlie

Every time Tomas and I said our goodbyes, I felt like I was leaving a part of myself behind. The pain seemed never ending.

It was as painful as the couch I slept on every night.

The first thing I did to distract myself was buy a new sofa for Mom's house. She didn't complain at all when I left to purchase a pullout bed from the local furniture place. The new one was plain beige, but it was as comfy as a cloud.

I still didn't sleep well the next night either. Or the next. Even after cleaning up a single corner in Mom's messy bedroom. The next morning I drifted back and forth between my new bed and the window near the kitchen table. I wasn't sure what I was looking for outside. Did I expect Tomas to show up after what I'd said to him a few days ago?

I kept checking my phone too, even turning off the lock screen so I could see a message immediately.

Mom caught me sitting on the couch staring out the window. "I thought I didn't move all that much," she grumbled.

"I'm just a little tired."

She ambled over to the fridge and grabbed a bottled water. She picked up my phone and tried to use it. There wasn't much to see. Just my text message screen.

"Can I help you find something?" I asked her a few minutes later.

"Oh, I wanted to see those photos again."

Oh good, I thought with relief. *A welcomed distraction.*

I brought up the pictures again. We laughed for a while and talked about the failed attempt for Rutger Rose to play the opening for a Dire Straits concert. According to Mom, the fans at that venue just didn't recognize their talent.

Seeing her smiling face made me feel bold for once. "Hey Patty, could you look this way and show me your best Rutger Rose manager face?"

I placed the camera in front of us for a selfie. At first, she wrinkled her nose at the idea, but I kept smiling and waited. The straight line of her lips curved into a grin and she brought her cheek close to mine. After a few clicks, I had my first pictures of me and my birth mom.

By the time I sat back down I realized she'd checked out my text messages instead of my web browser. What had she been looking at?

A week later, everything seemed to be back to normal, except I woke up to a quiet house. I checked Mom's room and found it empty. In a panic, I searched everywhere, even driving around the neighborhood until I found her at the local bus station. She stood in the long ticket line. All she had on her was a purse. No suitcase.

"What in the *hell* of God's green earth are you doing here?" I hissed.

"I'm buying a ticket. What does it look like?"

I was dumbfounded at this point. "You just had bowel surgery for cancer a month ago. Do you think Dr. Craft would approve?"

"I could give a shit," she grunted.

A few others in the line chuckled. I didn't find the situation as amusing. "So you just woke up and thought it would be a great idea to up and leave?"

"I used to do this all the time."

"Well, you're not twenty anymore."

"And you're a bossy roommate."

I sighed, considering other solutions as if she were a fussy hotel customer. "How about we talk about a trip after Dr. Craft approves? A Rutger Rose road trip?"

"Maybe." Her shoulders sagged a bit. She'd done too much already. Since she wasn't in the best shape to argue she begrudgingly followed me.

I drove her back to the house, but apparently we weren't done arguing yet.

"Why do you want to stay with me when you can have something better for yourself?" she griped.

"I do have something better. I have you now."

She made a rude gesture. "You were an assistant manager at a fancy hotel and now you're cleaning up after me, a person who is nobody and you think *this* is better?"

"To me, it's better." My voice was rising higher and higher. "You have no right to tell me that spending time with you isn't worth it. You lost that right when you abandoned me." I snorted. "You can't even abandon me again right. You just left the house with a hole-filled purse and you forgot half of your medicine."

"Those bottles are empty," she grunted.

We grew silent for a bit. I was still mad she'd pulled this

shit because she wanted to push me away again. *And I wondered where I got the urge to run away from?*

I took a few deep breaths and calmed myself. I *chose* to stay here. I left the man I'd loved for over half my life to be with the person I've always needed in my life. This was an opportunity I refused to waste.

Mom finally spoke. "I was never meant to be a mother."

"Well, sometimes we don't have a choice in the cards life deals us. You had me and now you're stuck with me."

"I don't have to be," she whispered. "You can get the fuck out."

"Make me." Mom had apparently eaten bullshit for breakfast.

"I'll call the police on you."

"Good, then they can see this place and you can march your stubborn self straight into protective care."

Her face contorted into an angry grimace. "Can't you see I want you to be happy," she bit out. "You can do all the things I wasn't able to do. You can have a family, maybe more."

"Don't you think I can do that with you in my life, too?"

"All you do is sit on that goddamn couch and look at your phone."

I sucked in a deep breath. "Oh, c'mon!"

"It's true." She placed her hand on me. The first time she'd ever done that. "You're hurting and I'm letting you stay that way."

"I'm not."

"A long time ago, I chose Frank and I saw so many places. I wish I could have seen Europe, you know? Seeing the US was nice and all, but I dream bigger than that."

She pushed me a bit. "I could've worked at the local meat packing plant, but I chose *him*. Now look at you. Are you running again, too?"

I was running away from Tomas. I was a professional at it, but I chose a better option. "I chose to run to *you*."

She touched my face and ran her palm down my cheek. Damn, having my mom touch me was all I'd ever wanted. "I've been here for fifty years. I'll be here for twenty more thanks to Dr. Craft."

"I'm still not going anywhere," I bit out.

"Just think about it, Carlie."

"Uh, huh."

She frowned. "I can be a nagging bitch."

"Can be?"

"Promise me you'll think about it."

I'd already turned him away and he planned to sell the building. For all I knew, the ink on the paperwork had dried already.

I nodded. "I'll think about it, Mom."

THE NEXT MORNING, I woke up and glanced at my phone again. No new messages from Tomas. A quick search on the Internet didn't reveal any information about a sale of the Goodfellow Tower Hotel but why would any sale go public until the company released the information.

Forget about him, Carlie.

So I freshened up first. On the way to the bathroom, I glanced in her room to see Mom on her side again. At least she hadn't run away.

I brushed my teeth. For the first time, I noticed that half of the bottles were empty. Damn, she did have a point there. I chuckled. I grabbed an empty bottle of painkillers and walked into the bedroom to wake her up.

"You win, Patty. They're empty." I touched her side, but she didn't stir.

Just another morning I'd have to drag her into the bathroom.

"You tired, sleepyhead?" I touched her hand, and it was cold.

Oh, God no . . .

"Momma . . ." My voice cracked as I reached for her to turn her over.

She wasn't breathing.

"Mom . . ." I scrambled to feel for a pulse, but her chest was silent.

"God, not now. Not now." I perched over her and began CPR. Two breaths. Five chest compressions. Countless times I'd practiced this procedure for emergencies like this one, but I never imagined I'd be doing it to my mother.

She still didn't respond.

"Goddamn it, you better wake up!" I was crying now, but Mom didn't move.

I grabbed my phone. Somehow I dialed the number I'd called numerous times at the hotel, but never for myself.

"911," the dispatcher said through my din. "What is your emergency?"

"Please . . ." I couldn't seem to find my breath. Black circles danced along my vision. "Come to 88 . . ." My throat was closing up. I leaned over and sucked in a deep breath. With the first gust of air, I gave the address. "My mom is unresponsive with no pulse or heartbeat." I couldn't speak anymore. Only howl.

I barely heard the woman say help was on the way. I dropped the phone.

"I'm not giving up on you." I tried again and again until my arms grew tired and the sounds of the sirens grew louder. Eventually, all I could do was weep, wrap my arms around her, and lay my head against her shoulder.

That was the first and the last time I hugged her.

Chapter Twenty-Six

Tomas

For the longest time, she sat on the couch on the rooftop patio. The air up there was always comfortable, and on the clearest of days, the sky over the bay offered the best view.

An endless line of doctors tried to reassure Carlie, but none of the words ever sank in.

"You did a great job taking care of your mother, but she lost her fight with cancer," one of my private physicians said. *"Did she ever tell you her prognosis wasn't good in the first place?"* She was numb the whole time like she was now. *"Parents never tell their children the bad news until it's too late."*

I took her to the funeral home, her appointment with the bank to settle her mother's affairs, anywhere she needed to go.

A majority of the time, I did the talking. Seeing her just going through the motions tore into me.

~

MORE TIME PASSED, but Carlie didn't do much.

A call from Roland came at the best time: Carlie had a visitor from the hotel.

We were on the roof watching the TV under the pergola when one of my hotel guests, Carver Murphy, came by for a visit. We chatted on occasion about his business dealings in the Midwest and he was a decent guy. I wasn't sure why he wanted to see Carlie, though.

She didn't do anything special for our guest. Most of the time, Carlie was impeccable in makeup and dresses, but today she lounged in a T-shirt and a pair of jean shorts. The fuzzy bunny slippers were unexpected, as well.

"Hey, Carlie." Carver waved at her and she offered a small smile back.

"I thought you had left town on business," I asked him.

He glanced at Carlie, a morose expression on his face. "I was in Chicago for a while with a case, but I had to come back to Boston. This place is turning into a second home for me."

"Does that mean you might be settling down? Ending the single life?" she joked halfheartedly.

"I don't know about that. I've been a bachelor for a long time."

They sat in silence for a bit. He waited patiently for her to speak first.

"Have you been drinking your shakes?" she finally asked him.

"Those shitty things? Sometimes my cook makes them for me when I order something bad."

That made her smile for the first time in days. "I want a disgusting cheeseburger right about now. Something I'd regret later."

He laughed and she laughed soon after. It was good to see her smile.

"How are you holding up?" he asked her.

"I'm doing fine." The side of her mouth puckered as if she'd bit it. "Like you said, I take things one day at a time."

He nodded. "That's all we can do."

A cooking show appeared on the outdoor TV and Carver groaned. "You do know you're torturing yourself, don't you?"

I was thinking the same thing, but I'd kept that thought to myself since she showed some interest in it every now and then. Having her feel better was all that mattered to me.

"This channel is like crack," she replied. "They have a show about diners and drive-ins. Shows about barbecue. Shows about candy."

"But nothing on gluten-free dining?" Carver relaxed against the seat.

"Nope. But it doesn't matter. Celiac's disease isn't a life sentence or anything."

I got up to pour her some more green tea and a glass for Carver. Just hearing them banter back and forth was refreshing. I had yet to get her to open up like that for me —which meant she needed friends right now, too.

They were still going at it when I came back.

"You would either go into diabetic shock eating that cake or you'd be in the bathroom for days with a sugar-free one," Carlie said.

"I'd die a happy man."

"Cake should not be deadly."

We sat quietly watching TV for a while until Carver spoke again. "I'm glad I got a chance to help you find your mom."

"I am, too." She took a sip of her drink. "I didn't want to ask for help—from anyone—but you ignored my protests and made the impossible possible. Thank you."

"Thanks, Carver," I added.

"Naw, man. This one was on the house from the beginning. Your lady deserved to find her mom. I'm glad she had the chance to get to know her."

We finished watching a cooking show before Carver said his goodbyes. Carlie hadn't said much since we talked about her mom and she continued to be that way for the rest of the week.

October became November, and by that point, Carlie rarely left the hotel.

One morning, I found her lying in bed. On her cellphone were many messages from her friends. They had been reaching out to her, but she wasn't responding to them.

Instead of going to work that day, I curled up next to her and held her.

Chapter Twenty-Seven

Carlie

"Hey, Car."

Someone cuddled up behind me and ran her hand down the side of my face. It was Sophie. Penny lay down near my feet. In front, Griffin sat on the edge of the bed and took my hand.

Sophie's perfume filled my nose and I managed a small smile.

"Hey, Ashley," I said to her.

"Why haven't you called me back?" Sophie asked softly.

"Because I've been out of it."

"I was hoping for more than a text."

I sighed and the tears that always sat on the edge of my vision threatened to come again. "I just knew if I called you, I wouldn't be able to speak." I covered my mouth to stop myself from sobbing and failed.

"You don't have to talk, Car." She held me close and stroked the back of my head. When we were kids, I was the one who comforted her. This time it was her touch that calmed me. "You never have to talk."

Penny was already crying and I just lost it. All this week, I'd wanted to go back to the UK. I was tired of feeling tired. I just wanted to dig myself a hole and bury myself inside, but right now, at this very second, the chill along my back went away and the emptiness I'd once wanted to fill with family didn't feel as empty.

We sat like that for a while. I wasn't sure how long until Penny spoke. "You smell."

I laughed and Griffin did, too.

"You're such a bitch, Penny," he snorted.

"Well, she does." Penny got up and took Griffin's hand. "Let's go get some coffee while Sophie gets her ass out of bed. We can have lunch after she freshens up."

I'd forgotten about our family lunch we did once per month. We always got together, even when I was overseas and had to video chat while they ate.

I'd missed last month.

Apparently, they weren't going to let me miss today.

Sophie dragged me out of bed, made me take a long shower, and forced me to put on something other than yoga pants.

"You make a pencil skirt look good," Sophie said. "About as good as me. Maybe."

I gave her the finger.

"You have someone else to take care of that," she replied.

"Not lately."

She leaned in and kissed my cheek. "You don't need *that* right now, but he's there for you if you need him. He's the one who called us over."

"Are you serious?"

"Yeah. So we're here to take you out to get some chow."

Sophie fetched some heeled sandals for me and put them on my feet. My toenails were atrocious.

"Thanks, Soph."

I was tearing up again, but this time I was content.

Her smile said it all. "Always."

THE MONTHLY LUNCH with the crew had been a long-standing tradition that started back when there had been over seven of us. As time had passed, Lillian had moved off to Florida, I'd left for the UK, and Sophie told me Mackenzie had simply disappeared for places unknown. Which was unusual since we'd been there for each other growing up. For the past couple of years, I'd attended our monthly lunch through a tiny screen on my smartphone. Seeing everyone up close and personal was nice.

We could've gone anywhere in town, but Tomas had shoved an American Express Centurion into my hand with a warning: enjoy a nice lunch or I'd receive a punishment like no other. As much as I needed a distraction to make the pain go away, the idea of going on a dick diet was worse so I relented.

What better way to spend hundreds of dollars than to eat lunch at the restaurant on Dante's Second Floor? I wasn't an employee anymore, but a paying customer who knew the perks. One of them being the ambiance. Just the view alone would make our meal much more *interesting*. The look on my friends' faces after the tour was totally worth it. Once we sat down and a server took our order, I was pleased to see Penny was speechless. For about five minutes.

SHAWNTELLE MADISON

"Why didn't I know about this place?" Penny whispered to Sophie.

"Because you can't afford a hotel that charges over a thousand dollars per night," Sophie replied. "I might have to plan a weekend getaway with Xavier."

I chuckled as a server brought us some water.

Penny pursed her lips. "I have a savings account for this kind of thing. If I'd known this was the view . . ." Our server, one of the more handsome staff members named Chris, had caught Penny's eye.

And, as if right on cue, Mr. Frasier was walking Millicent. He spotted me and strolled over.

"Ms. Jason, I haven't seen you in so long," he said with a bright smile. "I was worried you quit."

I smiled at him. "I did, Mr. Frasier, but I guess I can't stay away forever."

Today was just another afternoon for him and his pet. "Hopefully, I'll see more of you. My Millicent asked about you the other day."

Griffin couldn't keep his eyes off Millicent. Most men couldn't. Today she wore a golden leash and bright red garter belts. Every time she shifted, a tiny bell around her neck jingled.

"How sweet of her." Since I'd started working here, I'd come to find the more permanent guests were pretty cool people. The ones who came and went were demanding, but the clients who stayed made this a worthwhile work place.

With a wave and a polite goodbye, Mr. Frasier left.

Griffin was still staring.

"You okay, Griff?" I asked, trying not to tease him too much.

"Damn, that *ass*," he murmured.

"I wish my tits were that perky," Sophie added.

210

"Xavier can buy you some," Penny quipped.

Sophie giggled.

Just looking around the table I was already feeling a bit at ease, but another feeling crept into my stomach. One I faced from the time I woke up until the moment I lay down to go to sleep: an overwhelming need to run away.

The empty place in my heart was still raw with pain and being in Boston didn't seem wise. Originally I'd come here for my parents and now that they were both gone I wasn't sure what to do with myself. Every time I walked through downtown I saw reminders of my time with her. The doctor visits. The restaurants where we ate. Right now I just couldn't take it anymore. I thrived on the run and this place held me down.

As our food arrived everyone dug in, but I only had a single bite of my lobster bisque. Griffin had stars in his eyes while he inhaled his massive filet wrapped in bacon. Sophie and Penny were comparing the length of their rainbow trout portions to porn star penises. For goodness sake, I should be laughing and joking with them.

But I couldn't and dragging this decision along would only make things harder.

I swallowed down the lump in my throat. "There's something I need to say."

They gazed at me with concern.

"What's up?" Sophie asked.

"I've decided to go back to the UK." I forced myself to look at them. "Just until I can clear my head."

I waited for the protests—that was what they did when I told them I wanted Sophie to move to the UK with me, but they merely nodded—except Penny.

"I don't want to see you go, but I understand," Sophie finally said. "What you're feeling is still raw and it will be for a while. You need to do what is best for you."

"So you're just going to leave again?" Penny snapped. "I know you. It's not for a while. I hate to be the one who yanks out the damn-bitch card, but somebody needs to say something."

"Penny," Griffin warned.

"Don't." Her index finger went up to silence him and then she turned back to me. "I shouldn't be surprised you're pulling this shit. Running away is what you're good at doing."

"Fuck you," I bit out.

"Oh, *fuck* you back." She threw a fry at me, but I didn't take the bait to all-out fight. "Yes, you've taken a hit. The *absolute* worst. And yes, you need time, but damn it, there's no *reason* for you to leave. You need us. We need you."

I crossed my arms, swallowing away the growing fury rising in my stomach. I focused on the windows across the vast room. Maybe the calming skyline would keep me from tackling her ass. If I looked at her, I'd hurt her as much as she was hurting me. "I don't have to *have* a reason. I can't stay here anymore. It hurts."

She blew out a breath. "That's real life. Real life fucking hurts. With your family you get the good and the bad. We want you here so we can be there for you."

I didn't want to *wait* it out. Now that my feelings were out in the open, a weight had lifted off my shoulders. "What if I don't care anymore about whether I get the good or the bad? What if I'm worn so thin, I want to scream at the idea of looking at anything that reminds me of what I've lost." I tossed my napkin beside my bowl. "I'm done. I've been done."

I got up and stormed out of there. If I didn't leave, I'd say something I'd regret.

Chapter Twenty-Eight

Carlie

I f I stayed another hour in Boston, my head was gonna explode. A quick search on my phone confirmed a red-eye leaving Logan International at ten tonight. There were five seats free and I had a ticket in my purse ready to go. All I'd have to do was grab my shit in the penthouse and leave.

And yet leaving after everything I'd gone through with Tomas made me pause in the elevator going down. I closed my eyes and couldn't shut out what Penny had just said: *Running away is what you're good at doing.*

As angry as I was with her right now, she had a point.

The elevator reached the lobby and I pressed the button to go to the third-floor offices.

I couldn't leave like this—now that Tomas and I had figured things out—I had to let him know I was heading overseas for a while. He deserved that much.

I reached his office and Wendy let me in with a nod. There he was, sitting behind his desk, unaware of the turbulent emotions crashing into me. I wanted to climb into his lap and cry until I didn't hurt anymore.

Just one look at my face, and he approached me. "What's wrong?"

My mouth opened and closed. How the hell did I tell him I wanted to leave? After everything I'd been through, he'd been there each minute, each second. My heart hurt, but I had to speak.

"I need to go back home." A tear fell down my cheek and I didn't stop it. "Just for a little while."

"Is there a problem in London? I can call—"

I sniffed and tried to find my voice. "No, everything's fine with my business. I'm the one who isn't fine."

He drew me into his arms and I collapsed against him. Crying again was something I didn't want to do anymore.

"Don't fret, Gingerbread," he said softly. "We don't have to stay here. How about a weekend in New York?"

The breath I meant to exhale got caught in my chest. "Not New York. Much farther—"

"You're not leaving me," he said, his voice like stone. "Not anymore."

"Then what else can I do?" I was wheezing now. "There's this pain right here." I touched my heart. "And leaving seems like the only thing that makes sense. It's always been that way."

I searched his face. Unable to stop myself, I brushed my fingertips along the hard lines of his jaw to his full lips. "I can't stay here anymore."

"Then *we* don't have to stay."

"What are you saying?"

"That I love you, Gingerbread." He gently kissed my lips. "We'll see this through. I'm personally assessing two sites in a week or two. I can move the date up. Let's leave now."

He never let me go after that. Not while he called Wendy to make arrangements for the private jet flight to Heathrow International. Or when he called Saul to prepare his home in London.

I was going home soon, but the love of my life was coming with me.

~

THE MINUTE the jet set down at Heathrow, the tension in my stomach eased.

It was hard to describe. Once I got off the plane and we reached his tri-level brick home northwest of London, I felt so much better. Tomas and time would heal me and I'd head back to Boston when I cleared my head.

Now that we were here, naturally, I was curious as to where he stayed while he visited the UK. Had he ever been here when I lived here?

Compared to his modern penthouse, the stately home behind the gated entrance seemed laid back. Ivy covered parts of the front and the arches over the windows were practically whimsical.

"You hungry?" he asked me as we entered the massive kitchen. He checked the fridge and I peeked behind him to see it full of food.

"Why don't we go out tonight?" I'd kill for some pub food.

He frowned. "I was hoping we could eat in tonight like we did the other time. Just me and you. A couple of movies. Some popcorn and pizza." He kissed my lips and wrapped his arms around me and I felt so calm. I could get used to feeling this way all the time.

"We're back in London and you want to spend the

evening watching movies? Why not go out for drinks?" He
drifted to my neck to kiss my pulse point.

"We could make a movie?" His gaze darkened.

"A *Star Wars* movie?"

"I could show you my light saber."

I laughed. "Will you be my Han Solo?"

"Damn right I will be. Although I think Chewbacca
might be what you'd like."

"Tall and hairy." Having him close to me like this set
me at ease. Sparks danced in his eyes and I didn't want this
warm feeling to end. I finally had him on my turf.

He kissed my neck again and lifted me onto the desk.
Our kiss deepened and my stress melted away. Only Tomas
made me feel this way.

Then he began making snorting noises like Chewbacca. "I can do this until you give in . . ."

"Fine, then we'll watch a few movies after I get back."

"Where are you going?"

"To my old flat. I should check it out."

"I could have someone check it out for you, if
you want."

I shook my head. "Some time alone will do me some
good. I also have a few text messages to read. Most of
them are pissed-off messages from Penny."

He placed his hand along my cheek and stroked the
skin gently. I wanted more, but didn't say such. "Take my
B.M.W. then. Don't stay away long, Gingerbread."

The drive to my old flat in West Smithfield was a good
one. Driving through the outskirts of London could do that
to you. I'd invested so much money settling here, including
getting an apartment that most people couldn't afford. I
had been lucky that an old client of mine from the US was
selling his home. The place had three bedrooms and he

gave me a great price on it, as long as I let his cousin from Canada stay over the summer.

That was the kind of deal I didn't mind at all.

My home was in one of the many historic places in the northeastern part of London. I was within walking distance to the Museum of London and there was nothing better than watching snow fall on St. Paul's Cathedral during the holidays. As much as I would've liked to live in a crib like Tomas's, I couldn't afford a multi-million-pound home. This city definitely wasn't welcoming unless you had cash to burn. When I came a few years ago, I had plenty to start out my new business. Then I saw the cost of living and most of my savings quickly faded away.

My flat was quiet, though. I entered the living room first. Everything was as tidy as Paulie had left it. The summer had ended and he wasn't living here anymore. As I looked around at my place, my heart caught in my throat. My mom would've liked it here, especially since she liked to travel.

I wish I could have seen Europe, you know? she'd said. *Seeing the US was nice and all, but I dream bigger than that.*

I sucked in a breath as I left my purse on the counter and looked out the kitchen window. Beyond the backyard was a field where kids played soccer. I'd traveled to many countries as a part of my job. I'd seen things, eaten things. I'd wanted her to get better so that she could experience those things with me.

You're back at square one, Carlie. Just on a different game board. In my purse I took out the selfie picture I'd taken with her. Instead of the overwhelming sadness, a spark of hope passed through me. I was back in the UK. Maybe I could get back on track too, and kick a few asses.

Mom wouldn't want anything less for me.

I WAS KNOCKING out a bunch of phone calls and emails with old acquaintances, but a single text message sat unanswered on my phone for the last twelve hours:

When are you going to contact Penny?

The message from Sophie mocked me every time I checked my smartphone. How did she even know Penny and I were fighting? Well, Sophie did live with her.

I sighed. Yes, we'd fought, but our fight didn't compare to when we got into a fistfight at sixteen over a broken gold necklace, or the time when she abandoned me to avoid a double date with two guys at eighteen. I barely knew them, by the way, and I still got pissed thinking about it. But Penny was my girl. My partner in crime who called me up to tell me how Sophie was doing when Sophie got too busy to call me. When I first moved to London, she'd texted me every other day about her zany phone sex customers. Even when I was with my mom, she kept up her end when I'd faltered with mine.

Now she'd gone silent since I'd left.

Being the bigger person should be easy with our long history, but I'll be honest. It took me three hours to finally send a single text:

We need to talk.

Then I waited. And waited some more. After two hours, I wasn't surprised. Right now it was mid-morning in Boston. She had to be up by now to work a shift—which mean she was ignoring my ass.

Fine. Two could play this game. I pulled out my laptop and visited her work website. What I did know was she worked as an independent contractor for a phone sex company out of California. What I didn't know was the phone number: 1-900-COME-NOW.

Not the most creative number, but I managed to dial without laughing. Once the call went through, the menu options ranged from casual chat—yeah right—to light BSDM to the kinkier aspects of BDSM. I didn't know what Penny specifically offered, but I did know her professional name there: *Pretty Penny*.

With a devilish grin, I slid into a slot for *Pretty Penny* and waited, listening for the click.

She answered soon after. "Hi, this is Pretty Penny . . ." she purred.

I had to admit, having never heard her in action, her smooth, melodious voice gave me tingles. "Hey, Penny."

The face-smack silence on the other end of the line was expected.

Just not for two minutes straight. This was an international phone sex call, after all.

"Look, I'm sorry," I finally said.

"Whatever."

"I shouldn't have left like that." Yep, I was seriously apologizing over a phone sex hotline.

"Hmm-mmm."

"What I should have done was climb across that table and kick your ass," I grated.

She snorted.

I settled back in my office chair and curled my legs under me. "But I really do need some time to clear my head. Boston has too many painful memories right now."

Forever stubborn, she didn't answer.

My voice rose. "Damn it, Penny, I'm being the adult and apologizing instead of sending you a text message. At least say something."

"No."

"Fine," I grumbled. "I've said my piece and I'll wait until you forgive me."

"It's your dime," she said stiffly.

I sighed. Time to pull out the big guns. "Since you're so mad, I guess I'll have to keep Carver's phone number to myself."

"You think I need his number?"

I laughed. "You haven't seen what I've seen." Like Carver without a shirt going for a morning swim . . . "He's a really nice guy. Tattoos and muscles for days. Also, I know for a fact that he's *single*."

Just one look at Carver's gray-blue eyes, full lips, and bronze skin was more than enough to leave her hooked. She grumbled a bit then blurted, "I guess I can accept your apology for now—but you can't just walk away anymore."

"I agree." We both were quick to tell it like it is—a trait that made us abrasive to others but bonded us tightly together.

Now that we had cleared things up, I smiled, but I wasn't letting things go without a few parting words. "So . . . umm . . . are you gonna hook me up so this call is free?"

NOW THAT I'D resolved things with Penny, I could spend a relaxing evening with Tomas watching a soccer match between Manchester United and Chelsea. I practically gorged myself on fish and chips. Ever the miracle worker, Tomas had the chef whip me up a fabulous meal.

While we ate, I couldn't help but feel *normal*. Was this what it was like for regular couples? It wasn't like I hadn't dated before, but dating for me was nothing as simple as dinner together.

I looked briefly at Tomas. He pushed some popcorn into my mouth and I grinned like a fool.

"So who are you cheering for?" he asked.

"Chelsea, of course."

"You're kidding, right?"

"Maybe I should be asking you that question."

"I don't know if I can let you stay here if you keep talking like that. The Goodfellows have supported the Red Devils for decades."

I smiled at him in the coyest manner. "And I've lived here for several years and I own six Chelsea T-shirts."

"That doesn't mean you *know* any better."

I punched his arm for good measure. "I happen to know a lot. Like you need to offer better guest services in your hotel rooms."

He rolled his eyes. "Have you seen what some of the folks on the twenty-second floor have ordered?"

"I'm not talking about that floor—I'm talking about regular guest rooms. The ones who call the customer service desk all the time asking about dining and entertainment options."

He crammed a handful of popcorn into his mouth. Maybe so he wouldn't have to answer. "Have you ever thought about how much that would cost to develop?"

I laughed. "It's just a thought. Can you imagine how much revenue you could generate from touch screens in the rooms?" I kept going as ideas flooded my head.

He ran his hand down my arm. A definite attempt at distracting me. "I have ideas, too . . ."

"You keep touching me," I whispered. "If you look away, your team is going to lose."

"Well, at least somebody is gonna score tonight."

I laughed. His caresses grew a bit bolder and his hand slid down the side of my breast. I sighed. The couch cushions were so comfortable. His touch was light, but I knew Tomas. Light wasn't his thing. I waited for him to grow bolder, to grip me tighter, but the laziness of our kiss grew longer.

His tongue was bold, not tentative like mine, gliding against mine until my toes curled. He turned over me, his body over mine. His spicy scent filled my nose and I couldn't do anything except wrap my arms around his waist.

Everything about him was responsive from the way he nibbled along my neck and then ventured back to my mouth. I reached under his shirt and ran my hands along the hard muscles underneath. When I rubbed over his nipples, he twitched and I grinned. Tomas always had a thing for me touching him there. I jerked my hips, but he kept kissing me. So I grabbed a nipple between my fingertips and pressed hard. He hissed in response, his gaze darkening.

"Are we just making out or fucking?" I finally asked.

"Do you want to be fucked?" His smile was devilish.

"Again and again."

He pulled off my shirt first. The cool air in the room hit my back. Next came my pants. When I reached for him, he pushed my hands away.

"Not yet, *Coração*."

He kissed my inner thigh and came up to capture my lips again. Every place he sucked sparked heat inside of me until I was writhing for more.

He was teasing me; it was quite apparent by the time he tugged off my panties. He turned over onto my back as Manchester scored a goal.

"Damn it—" My grunt turned into a moan as he slid a finger inside of me.

His tongue slid up my back. "I love this phoenix tattoo. I remember when you got it."

"It hurt like a motherfu—" He added a second finger, stretching me wonderfully.

"How many hours?" He was casual about his conversation as his lips worked over me and his fingers drove me toward a hard orgasm.

"Three days," I panted. "Each of them a four-hour session." I couldn't stop the moan rising from the back of my throat. The sweet feeling I couldn't contain as he filled me again and again. The tension in my limbs grew harsh and I cried out his name.

But he wasn't done with me yet. He kissed lower along my back. "And how about this tattoo?"

I was wet with perspiration now. I was still lying on my stomach and I leaned my head against the cushion, barely able to move.

"Which one?" I murmured.

He recited the Latin on my back: *Faber est suae quisque fortunae.* He pushed into me hard and deep. I shuddered from the sweet pleasure.

"Ah, that one. It means everyone is the creator of their own fate." I sucked in a breath. "It's inked under my skin so I don't forget."

He intertwined our fingers. "Is that your motto, Gingerbread?"

I expected him to pound into me, but his strokes were agonizingly slow against my ass.

Does he really want me to talk right now?

"Fuck, baby, you're so tight." Apparently, he was having trouble speaking, too.

Again and again, he pulsed inside of me, marking me as his in a gentle manner we had hardly explored before. I thought I wouldn't feel the rising pleasure I felt now, but I couldn't contain the long moan that was wretched from my mouth.

Not far from us, the TV continued to blare with the closing minutes of the game. I could barely hear anything about the penalty kick as his stroke deepened and my climax was coming again.

"Carlie," he moaned.

I loved hearing him call my name. "Say it again," I whispered.

"Carlie, I can't get enough of you."

He pressed me against the couch now and his grip on my hands tightened. He was pressing me into the cushions and I could barely breathe, but I was almost there again. He was almost there too, our bodies moving together as one. Him downward, me upward. We met in the middle, folding into each other as our bodies reached a blissful peak.

Once he finished, he sagged against me. I welcomed his weight. Especially the kisses along my damp brow.

"Your team won," he whispered in my ear.

"Maybe you should sell the stock you own."

He rose off me and looked at the television with distaste. "Good point."

I watched him walk off and enjoyed staring at his tight ass. He rarely worked out like he used to do when we were younger but he still had a body carved in steel.

I was practically exhausted, but somehow I managed to get up and get dressed again.

We watched a movie. After that, I drifted off into the best sleep ever.

There was something wonderful about sleeping in his arms back home. I didn't need to run away, I was back where I wanted to be.

Without a doubt, in the morning, I knew he'd be there.

Chapter Twenty-Nine

Carlie

Waking up late—without my army of clocks—gave me joy. Of course, Tomas was here for business, but since he controlled his own schedule, we toured a potential construction site in the Abbots Manor neighborhood after lunch.

I could get spoiled living like this.

I had to admit, the site was perfect and I could get used to having Tomas here with me. The Thames was a few blocks away and tourists could walk to Big Ben if they wanted. For someone of Tomas's standing, the place was ideal. As I watched Tomas look over plans and discuss construction details with his team, I inevitably asked myself: *what do you want to do?*

Was I happy to finally be with Tomas the way we were meant to be? *Undeniably, yes.*

I could even jump back into my concierge business and live the fast-paced life I had before. I was sure I could make a comeback, even after I'd hired someone else at such a great expense.

But the idea didn't excite me as quickly as I'd wanted it to. My happiest moment not too long ago had been when I was with my mom in that tiny cottage of hers and seeing Tomas. I smiled. That tiny, messy house and my mother had me questioning what I wanted to do.

Now that was unexpected.

The week stretched along and we spent less time alone as Tomas continued to have meetings with his planning team. Instead of letting me sneak away to connect with old business partners, Tomas dragged me along.

"Now that you're with me, I'm not letting you go," he'd say every morning.

I learned so much that week. So many things went into selecting a site for a new hotel and that didn't even include the particulars for the interior. As much as I tried to be a bystander, Tomas pulled me in whenever he could.

On Friday morning he seemed pensive as he drank a cup of black coffee. "What's on your mind, Goodfellow?"

"It's you."

"After what I did to you last night, I'd be on my mind, too."

He rolled his eyes. "I'm meeting with a few companies on Monday. I'd like for you to talk more about those ideas we discussed a week ago."

"What ideas?" I *knew* very well what he was talking about.

"Running a concierge business is nice and all, but you have the potential to do so much more." He looked dead serious. "Your concierge business should be a *subdivision* of a guest services company."

Me, start up a guest services company? The very idea seemed too big for me to grasp. It wasn't as if I didn't know about business licenses, or rules and regulations in the UK, but the very idea of creating a company, or even an empire like what Tomas had scared the shit out of me.

"You look like I asked you to cross the Atlantic in a paper boat." He stroked my cheek. "All I'm asking you to do is come up with a presentation. Not save the world."

Reluctantly, I agreed to finish one by Monday. As I worked on the presentation though, I wondered if Tomas had found an underhanded way to keep me distracted, but by the time I really sat down and thought about what I could do everything clicked.

And boy did I get excited.

The weekend flew by and I couldn't wait.

Until I had to speak in front of ten people who looked like they were ready to swallow me whole. Even the state-of-the-art offices where the meeting was held didn't seem to tamper down my fear. Somehow, I shoved the apprehensive Carlie in the corner and began the speech I prepared.

"Having a qualified concierge team is pivotal, but the human touch isn't always necessary." I held up a standard guidebook that came with any hotel. It wasn't hard to find one in piss-poor shape. "Imagine that you're visiting a hotel somewhere in a major city and you see this." I had Tomas's assistant Wendy pass out additional copies to the planning team.

"It's full of places to eat and things to do. That's great, but frequently, our customers still go to the concierge desk and ask what's good. There's also the inherent printing costs of these booklets. If you want to go upscale, I'm thinking terminals in the rooms." I brought up my presentation on the overhead screen and Tomas smiled.

This is just the beginning, babe.

"With a system in place, not only can you easily update the content, but you can work with local companies to advertise and share potential revenue." Once I said the money word, I had everyone's attention.

I even had tablets with sample layouts. All weekend, I let myself go nuts planning out this venture and I felt like I'd only touched the potential of what could be done. If I could secure contracts with major hotels, this software could go from the corkboard to real life.

After the meeting was over, Tomas and I ate lunch at a high-end French cuisine restaurant downtown off Portland Place. I refused to ask him about how his team took my presentation, but I was curious about what they thought of the London site.

"So what was the final consensus?" I asked him.

"We won't be making any decisions until we evaluate Seoul."

I nodded. Which meant he'd be leaving again for who knew how long.

"You're coming with me right?" he asked.

"To be honest, I'm rather excited about this consulting firm idea you've tossed in my lap." I took a sip of my martini as I tried to find a way to say the obvious. "And my old clients have found me."

He didn't miss a beat. "So, I've noticed. Are you open for business again? Will I need to line up behind the rest of your customers for your attention?"

"Not exactly . . ." I was all grins.

We ate for a while, but the obvious conversation hung between us until I gave up and spoke. "How long would you need to evaluate the site in Seoul?"

"Five months. Much longer than here. It's a new market I haven't tapped into yet. So far I've read over the initial reports and things look promising."

Five. Months.

I had trouble swallowing my food. Could I do this again? Leave behind a business to go with Tomas?

"Carlie, I feel like you're slipping away from me again."

"I'm not."

"You're lying to me, Gingerbread."

"Yes, I am." I bit my lip. "Can I have some time to think about it?"

~

THREE DAYS.

That was all he gave me to make a decision.

Life is all about obligations, Carlie. Someday when you're in my shoes, you'll be forced to do the same.

No shit, Sherlock. Back when I was nineteen, all I thought was that he was another golden-parachute college kid who couldn't stand up to his dad and live his own life. I was bitter back then, but now I was bitter about myself.

I was back in the office at the flat again, feeling at home with my favorite tea and a box of Barkat bars from the local store. The radio was on and snow was falling outside. And yet, I stared out that window again.

I'd fucked up. Yet again.

My phone rang for the fourth time today and I picked up.

"Oh, Miss Carlie, I finally got ahold of you."

I smiled hearing an old friend's voice. Lucy Hamilton was the bored housewife of a transportation business owner, and she spent more time trying to climb the social ladder than pay attention to her juvenile delinquent children. "Miss Lucy, how are you, dear?"

We spent the next ten minutes going over niceties. "So what can I help you with?"

"Oh, the old biddy who wanted the yacht club meeting isn't happy anymore about the last party I organized for her. Do you really have pull with the Shelton Club?"

I did have pull, but I had been out of the scene for a little while. All the elbows I used to rub might've gone sour.

"I still do." Why deny that time might've passed.

I slid into the role I used to have easily. I hustled. That was what I was good at doing.

Lucy giggled in a high-pitched manner. "I will bring you the world on a platter if you can help me."

"How did you know I was in town?"

"I've got sources. One of my minions saw you walking hand in hand with Tomas Goodfellow on Market Street. Are you two an item now?"

Damn, her minions were good.

She continued. "My first thought of course was, is Carlie back in town to stay again?" she said.

Maybe.

"I could get you work for the next few months if you wanted."

The familiar thrill coursed through me. I could have what I wanted again. But then I remembered as she spouted all her busy clients how overwhelmed I'd felt. The growing tension that coincided with my stomachaches.

I'd sat in this very chair eating crisps agonizing over how the hell I could clone myself or get Sophie here so she could help me work. What the hell was I doing?

Hadn't Dr. Craft told me I needed to take better care of myself?

I looked at the cupboards where all my old food still sat. Row after row filled with bad habits.

As soon as my conversation was over with Lucy, I got up and fetched a garbage bag. Ten minutes later, I tossed out everything I shouldn't eat. Not that I had the temptation anymore, but the point was made. It was time to do the right thing.

I looked over my contacts in my phone. Row after row of connections. I used to look at this list with pride, but they were nothing more than names.

How does this thrill compare to when you are with Tomas?

The thrill didn't even come close. All these feelings I had for him transcended this job.

So what the hell are you going to do?

Three days later, I made my decision and ended up at the nearest pub around seven. A place called Bennington Brewery on the corner of Baker Street and Cambridge Ave. Local factory workers came here after work to play darts and have a pint or two. On a nice cold evening like this one, I liked the atmosphere compared to most of my upper-crust customers.

I could sip my drink and listen to people talk about average lives.

I sent a text to Tomas: *Meet me in front of the Blythe Hotel.*

~

Tomas

When I got the text from Carlie, my hand stiffened around the phone.

Was this where things were going? Would I meet "Grace" again? Maybe "Patience" this time? Carlie's time was up and my flight to Seoul was leaving tonight.

I still did what she wanted, since I had been waiting for her answer for the past couple of days. All the distractions of looking for another site was nothing compared to the sinking feeling like she was slipping out of my hands again.

As I walked toward the Blythe Hotel, I kept seeing her

face when we were eating dinner earlier this week. The way her eyes sparkled as she talked about staying here and building up her business again. We could try to make it work long distance, but I knew us. I knew how we functioned.

We used each other as needed and spit each other back out.

She went her way and I did the same.

I turned the corner at Baker Street and there she was in trousers and a white coat that fit along her waist. She was quite beautiful with her red hair gathered up along her neck in a braid. She looked as young as the day when I first saw her standing on the corner near Central Park.

I approached her and she smiled.

"Hi, Tomas."

"Hey, Gingerbread."

That made her smile wider and my heart squeezed thinking about what she'd say to me.

But then she turned away from the hotel.

"Where are you going?" I asked. I pointed toward the Blythe.

"This way. C'mon, Goodfellow. You're wasting a perfectly good evening."

So I followed her down the street and she ventured into a pub called Bennington Brewery. We sat at the bar.

"Have you ever been here before?" she asked me.

"Never." The bartender asked what we wanted and she ordered two pints of the house special.

"Can you drink this?" I asked her.

"Not really, but tonight is special."

I shook my head. "Not anymore." I pushed the drink back. "Got anything gluten-free?"

The bartender made a face. "We don't have any."

"I'll be okay, Tomas. Just let me have a bit." She smiled at me and the way the lights overhead hit her hair, I had to comply.

"What are you doing?" I asked.

"Changing. This is my last day." She fished inside of her purse and pulled out a list. "These are all my favorite things. Tomorrow, I'm making a fresh start."

"A fresh start?"

"I've been running away for a long time. All my life I've worked myself to the bone to climb out of the gutter I thought I grew up in."

I nodded.

"But I didn't start out in the gutter. I was born to a bass guitar player and his band manager. They traveled all over the US and saw the Grand Canyon before I even got out of diapers." She smiled again, her expression wistful. "All the time I thought I'd been abandoned, I hadn't been. My mom did what she had to because she didn't know any better. Even when I'd met her she was ill-equipped to be a mom."

"You grew up just fine in my opinion."

"Yeah, but I made assumptions. I assumed I'd be happy if I learned how your life was lived. I saw your life and thought you had it easy. I loved to please other people. Pleasing you gave me the most pleasure."

The drink in my hands cooled against my palm.

"At this point I'm going in circles and I can't keep doing that anymore. I can't keep running and trying to find what I thought I never had . . ."

"Love," I finished.

"Exactemente, Tomas."

I wanted to kiss her at that point. I fought the growing need to lean over and press my lips to hers.

"Love was always there waiting for me." She looked away, her face flush. "You were always waiting for me. I thought every time when we were together I could satisfy that itch, but scenes aren't enough." They were never enough.

"Why?"

"I always felt like I'd cut myself when we left each other behind. The pain never changed. If I walk out that door and go back to my old life, I'll be doing the same thing to myself."

I'd had time to contemplate the same. The moment I got on that plane to Seoul for five months, I would allow myself to fall into my job. That was what I did. Canceling everything though would be a big financial loss.

But what if I did something different and stayed with her tonight and finished this beer instead of getting on that flight?

She looked at my watch. "It's almost eight."

"Yes, it is." I smiled at her and she returned my smile.

"Your flight will take over eight hours to get to Seoul. And you probably have a meeting with your team in the morning."

I took a generous drink and even grabbed some nuts from a nearby plate. "Yes, it will take that long. And yes I do."

She played with her drink and didn't take a sip as she'd promised.

"I'm tired of letting you go," she admitted.

"Me, too."

"Then don't let me go." She pushed her drink my way and took my hand.

"How do we make this work?" I asked her.

"I've packed my bags. I was thinking if we left after you

234

finished my drink, we could catch that flight to Seoul." Her smile turned feline. "But since you happen to have a jet, I'm sure we could arrange another flight."

"I believe that's something I *can* do."

Chapter Thirty

Carlie

One year later.

After living in Seoul for the past year, I have to say I've never had a better city view than this one. For years, I've taken care of myself, but I rather liked this new arrangement: I lived with Tomas now while he constructed the Goodfellow Gangnam Tower Hotel.

Even I'm not a fool when it comes to enjoying what life has to offer. Why live alone and have a rooftop sweatbox apartment in Itaewon when I could live in a luxurious, ten-bedroom penthouse suite with Tomas in Gangnam? That was pretty much a no-brainer.

So I stayed and stared at the late night moon when I couldn't sleep. From my bed I had the best view of the Dongho Bridge and the Han River. Amber lights illuminated the girders while navy-blue lights cast a glow along the tall posts. It was breathtakingly beautiful.

Seoul shined in ways London and Boston didn't. The city pulsed as if it had a life of its own. Over the past year, I've explored South Korea's capital, from the amazing Bongeunsa Buddhist temple built in 794 a.d., to the exclusive luxury shopping district here in the affluent Gangnam neighborhood.

With time I could claim this city as my own, too.

An arm slipped around my middle and drew me back to Tomas's hard chest. Warmth enveloped me. "What are you doing up, Gingerbread?" the voice behind me asked.

"I'm daydreaming again. At night."

"Go back to sleep."

"I'm busy night dreaming."

"Most people dream while *sleeping*." He kissed the back of my neck, reminding me I'd made the best decision to stay.

"Sleeping is for amateurs."

I turned around to run my hands over his corded arms. I loved touching his skin. I brushed my lips against him. Not a kiss, but a hint of something more.

"Was that a dare?" he murmured. He kissed my lips, lingering long enough to show me how turned on he was.

"I'm daring you to fuck me right here," I boldly declared.

He chuckled. "As much as I'd like to bend you over near the window and show the world how insolent you've become, I'm thinking you'd prefer the bed. I like you in my bed anyway."

That got a groan of protest from me. Every now and then I went through an exhibitionist phase, but this was the one country where I had to behave. Tomas was always willing to give in to me, but apparently not tonight.

A year ago, we would've come to the bed as if playing out a scene. Now we lay face-to-face in *our* bed.

"Tomas, please love me," I whispered.

"Always."

No more Grace. No more Patience. We were Tomas and Carlie now. But we still satisfied each other's needs. Right beside our king-sized bed was a cedar box with a double-lock latch. From the box, he plucked out the nipple clamps and the bondage hemp.

No pockets needed for toys now.

He bound my hands at the wrists and then covered my body with his, our kiss stretching out until I thought my lips would be bruised. From my mouth he drifted downward, worshiping my body with each bite along my neck until his tongue flicked each nipple. A slow sensual stroke that made my toes curl.

Then he applied the clamps. I sucked in a breath. The pain blossomed into both bitter and sweet. With a dark glint to his eyes, he threaded a thin gold chain through my nipple rings, as well as the ring through my clit. He tugged twice on the chain and a shock pulsed from my breasts and shot straight to my pussy.

Damn. So. Good. I bit back the moan crawling up the back of my throat.

"Are you all right?" he asked. "I want to play some more."

"More please."

Watching my face all the while, he tightened the clamps a bit more—only to pluck them off again. One by one. Not too slow, not too fast. Before he added them back he lingered to kiss the stinging flesh. I fell into the beautiful space where only he and I existed. The place where he gave pain and I experienced it.

"My beautiful, Carlie." He untied me, removed the clamps, and lay between my legs.

The moment he sank into me, I was filled. I wrapped

my arms around his broad shoulders and accepted every-thing he gave me. Every deep stroke filled my soul and my heart. This was where I wanted to be.

His lips met mine. Tongues brushed against tongues and our bodies danced together as if we were constructing the most beautiful symphony.

His hips pumped faster and he grabbed my ass to deep-ened his stroke. My nipples stung from the clamps, but it was nothing compared to the rising heat inside of me. The pounding pleasure that rose every time he called out my name.

Sweat lined his brow. He was working hard this time. Pounding hard just how I liked it. This was my reward. The pain and then the pleasure.

My back arched and the tension along my stomach raced to my limbs and back. I screamed and he covered his mouth with mine.

~

Tomas

OUR BODIES FIT TOGETHER PERFECTLY. There was something beautiful about having her with me. We knew what each other needed. She didn't let me go until I climaxed inside of her.

We lay together for the longest time side by side.

With a yawn, she stretched out onto the crock of my arm. Her curly red hair slid like silk against my skin. Soon enough she dozed off, but I continued to lay there content and at peace. Just like her, I often dreamed at night while wide awake. Most of my thoughts were thankful in nature.

My love was with me now and I'd find her here in the morning, too.

Our beginning was innocent—now that I thought back it was bittersweet, too. Like those late summer dahlias. The flowers bloomed at the end of summer, but the moment of delight could last if you held onto the feeling for the rest of the year. Our love had been pure from the start, but time had darkened our fair skies to grey.

Over the years I learned time could take what was once pure and make it complete again through refinement. In the process of truly loving each other, we found each other once again. In the future, we'd have arguments and disagreements, but each one will make us closer. Stronger. And one thing will never change: we always find each other in the end.

Carlie smiled in her sleep. She wouldn't wake up any time soon. Things were different now—no more alarm clocks. Not that they worked for her anyway. She'd started her consulting business thanks to my investment, and soon enough, she'd be opening her office here in Seoul. So far I considered her company a valuable asset. Especially for my hotel in Boston.

I made Kraven the president over the hotel and management. He was overdue for finding his own way.

The hit to my portfolio took some adjustment, but with time I'd see back a high profit margin. Dante's Twenty-second floor made me a lot of money. Ending that arrangement to sell the hotel to someone else just because I needed a new toy wasn't looking beyond my needs.

Like Carlie, I was tired of running. I did want to forge my own path, but at this point, I wanted to make some-thing to grow into. Seoul offered that challenge to me. After that, who knew how the wind would blow.

I pulled her closer, and surprisingly, she woke up.

"If you keep doing this, how are you gonna get up tomorrow?" she asked me.

"I think we should sleep in. Then I can make you pancakes again."

She groaned. "You need a new recipe. Your last batch didn't taste too good."

"Work with me here, Gingerbread." So far, Korean cuisine worked out great for her lifestyle changes. Of course, having a personal chef helped in that regard.

"Not hard enough, Goodfellow. Let Raoul do the cooking." She snorted. "Have you cleared your schedule so we can attend Sophie's wedding next month?"

"I asked Wendy to make sure I'd be there. Maybe you should be asking yourself the same question."

"I don't forget things like that."

"Will she be upset we got married without your family being there?"

She pursed her lips as if deep in thought. The wedding ring I gave her three months ago in Thailand sat on her finger. This one was much bigger than the forgotten promise ring. "This won't be the first time I get a lecture from Sophie or Penny, but it doesn't matter. At the moment, it was the *right* thing to do."

Doing things on a whim was what Carlie did. When she told me yes, I didn't hesitate to have the ceremony. Now that I had her, I wasn't letting her go, but a part of me knew she regretted getting married without her close family.

"Why don't we do something small after Sophie gets married in Phoenix?" I suggested. Sophie, Penny, and Griffin had been there for her during the good times and the bad.

Slowly, she nodded. Sleepiness clung to her. "We could

make it a vacation. I know this great Japanese restaurant where we could have dinner."

"Fuck. No."

She smirked at me. "Are you saying you're not man enough to eat a fish's sperm sack?"

Instead of answering her, I captured her lips with mine. She giggled against my mouth and I knew I was in trouble, but Carlie was the kind of trouble I planned to keep. For a very long time.

About the Author

Shawntelle Madison is a Web developer who loves to weave words as well as code. She'd be reluctant to admit it, but if pressed, she'd say that she covets and collects source code. After losing her first summer job detasseling corn, Madison performed various jobs, from fast-food clerk to grunt programmer to university webmaster. Writing eccentric characters is her favorite job of all. On any given day when she's not surgically attached to her computer, she can be found watching cheesy horror movies or the latest action-packed anime. Shawntelle Madison lives in Missouri with her husband and children.

www.ingramcontent.com/pod-product-compliance
Lightning Source LLC
Chambersburg PA
CBHW021008120726
47905CB00009B/2905